Also by Ellen Hagan

· · · · · · · · · · · · · · · · · · · ·

Watch Us Rise (with Renée Watson)

Reckless, Glorious, Girl

ELLEN HAGAN

BLOOMSBURY
CHILDREN'S BOOKS
NEW YORK LONDON OXFORD NEW DELHI SYDNEY

BLOOMSBURY CHILDREN'S BOOKS
Bloomsbury Publishing Inc., part of Bloomsbury Publishing Plc
1385 Broadway, New York, NY 10018

BLOOMSBURY, BLOOMSBURY CHILDREN'S BOOKS, and the Diana logo
are trademarks of Bloomsbury Publishing Plc

First published in the United States of America in February 2021
by Bloomsbury Children's Books

Bloomsbury books may be purchased for business or promotional use. For information on bulk
purchases please contact Macmillan Corporate and Premium Sales Department at
specialmarkets@macmillan.com

Library of Congress Cataloging-in-Publication Data
Names: Hagan, Ellen, author.
Title: Reckless, glorious, girl / by Ellen Hagan.
Description: New York : Bloomsbury Children's Books, 2021.
Summary: Twelve-year-old Beatrice Miller copes with the ups and downs of friendships, puberty,
and identity, guided by the wisdom and love of her beloved mamaw and mom, the summer before
seventh grade.
Identifiers: LCCN 2020024837 (print) | LCCN 2020024838 (e-book)
ISBN 978-1-5476-0460-9 (hardcover) • ISBN 978-1-5476-0461-6 (e-book)
Subjects: CYAC: Novels in verse. | Adolescence—Fiction. | Mothers and daughters—Fiction. |
Family life—Kentucky—Fiction. | Friendship—Fiction. | Kentucky—Fiction.
Classification: LCC PZ7.5.H34 Rec 2021 (print) | LCC PZ7.5.H34 (e-book) | DDC [Fic]—dc23
LC record available at https://lccn.loc.gov/2020024837

Book design by Danielle Ceccolini
Typeset by Westchester Publishing Services
Printed and bound in the U.S.A. by Berryville Graphics Inc., Berryville, Virginia
2 4 6 8 10 9 7 5 3 1

All papers used by Bloomsbury Publishing Plc are natural, recyclable products made from wood
grown in well-managed forests. The manufacturing processes conform to the environmental
regulations of the country of origin.

To find out more about our authors and books visit www.bloomsbury.com and sign up
for our newsletters.

For Gianina Bazaz Hagan, Elinor Sferra Bazaz &
Miriam Dawson Hagan—
for all the mothering & grandmothering you all
did to raise me. Love, love.

Reckless,
Glorious,
Girl

Beatrice Miller's Burning Questions

Will Mom & Mamaw ever see me as more
than a little kid? Will they ever trust me?
Recognize my growing? See my evolution?
Witness my expansion?

I've been studying other words for "mature"
in our big ol' thesaurus & they include:
Evolve
Develop
Blossom
Ripen
Arrive.
Will those words ever happen to me?

How can I celebrate all of who I am?
Garden & Movie Lover
Bike Rider
Swim Teamer
Nacho Eater
Comic-Book Nerd
Superhero Obsessed
Mamaw & Mom Hugger
Late-Night Couch Cuddler.

Should I shine a light on all the parts

of me that no one can see?
Nervous
Anxious
Embarrassed
Awkward.
Maybe if I could share those feelings,
then people would see more of the real me.

Always, I'm wondering,
will Mariella, StaceyAnn & I ever be officially cool?
Not outskirts, outside, sideline cool
but ruling the school,
making all the jokes,
getting all the laughs,
full lunch table,
friends finding us after the bell rings.
You know, that kind of cool.
The kind that's smooth,
enters the room before you do.

Anyway, I've got about a trillion more questions,
but you have to start somewhere.

Backyard Daydreaming

You can find me swinging steady & slow,
my feet high in our tie-dyed hammock
('course it's tie-dyed—Mamaw wouldn't have it
any other way). Once I get a rhythm going,
my head clears right up. I'm not caught
in mistakes or hiccups from my past
& I'm not hung all the way up on my future,
who I am, who I'll be.
Just here, just now.
Mamaw says, "That's the good stuff,
your meditative state."
She says, "Empty your brain
and the world will come straight to you."

I have no idea what the heck she means.

But when she says, "Time is a construct,"
& I suddenly find myself swinging all afternoon long
with not one care in the whole wild world?
Well, then I'm pretty sure she knows
exactly what she's talking about.

Mamaw

Maa—almost like the sound of a goat baaing.
& "maw" like a mouth. Caw with an *M* sound.

Mamaw. Maaamaaaw. Mamawwww. Mamaw.

I say it like a chant or some spell I'm setting.
Never thought a thing about it being different
or weird or too country or too down South.

In the fifth grade, Shelby Perkins said, "Anyone
who calls their GRANDMOTHER MAMAW
or MEEMAW is a HILLBILLY." She was all the time
talking in capital letters at us. And by *us*,
I mean anyone who didn't live McMansion-style
or have the freshest sneakers, name-brand anything.
Anyone who didn't grow up with more & more.
I mean anyone who used the word "mamaw."
Shame filled me up.

"Welp, I guess I'm a hillbilly, then," StaceyAnn said,
sticking her chin all the way up.
"Besides, I bet my meemaw
could whoop your grandmother's butt any ol' day."
I gave StaceyAnn a look that said, *Stop talking!*
But she kept on. "Any name you give your granny

4

is the right one. You worry about your grandmother"
(This time she said it with a British accent.)
"And I'll worry about my meemaw."
(This time she slathered on the twang.)

We walked home laughing about our comeback
& StaceyAnn's sharp tongue, which she swears
she got straight from her meemaw. Lucky us.

My Room, My Sanctuary

"I wish my door had a dang lock," I holler out
to what feels like no one, since both Mom & Mamaw
are crooning their hearts out to "Baby Love,"
The Supremes turned all the way up. Record player
spinning. I'll bet I'm the only twelve-year-old who knows
how to use an old Victrola, & that's nothing to brag about.

StaceyAnn & Mariella are coming over for our weekly
summer sleepover, & I gotta get this room just right.

New purple bedspread with the solar system shining.
Bright yellow stars that Mariella will fall in love with.
Posters of Storm, Wonder Woman & Katana.
A few of the superheroes we love.
Thinking of my own superpowers
& how to make them come alive.
A big drawing of the astrological signs too.

Mariella is an Aries all the way. All floaty & dreamlike.
Connected to the sky & nowhere near earth.
StaceyAnn is a Sagittarius. Optimist. Freedom seeker.
She says it. And we believe her.

I'm a Scorpio. Everyone says I'm the
passionate,

intense,
wild one,
but I still haven't been able
to figure out exactly what that means
or who that is.

I pack up the last of my dolls, all their bottles,
blankets, baby clothes & plastic pacifiers.
Used to be we'd pull all those old toys out & play
like when we were kids, but lately
it's happening less & less.
I hold my favorite doll to my chest & my eyes fill up.
If Mamaw saw me, she'd say, "What has come over you,
sweet Beatrice?" But I already know.

It's the saying goodbye to the old me
while having no idea
who the new me even is just yet.

Doorbell Rings

Mariella & StaceyAnn race through the house.
Some things never change. That's for sure.
They give quick kisses to Mamaw & Mom
& throw open my door (see the no-lock situation).

They both *ooohhh* & *aaahhh* at my new setup,
pile on to the lime-green beanbags & kick back.
Like always, we make plans.

Mariella: finish work on our graphic novel,
Superhero Sisters Explore the Solar System.
I'm not sold on the working title, but we'll get there.
"I made some new sketches."
She pulls open her backpack & illustrations
come pouring out.

StaceyAnn starts next: work on some new songs.
"My dad taught me three new chords."
She pulls her smooth, sleek guitar from its case
& starts to strum. Never mind that all I can play
is the dang tambourine. StaceyAnn has enough
confidence & cockiness to make it all work.
She's sure we're gonna be musical superstars,
& while I'm a little less positive, I do love
singing at the tip-top of my lungs
when no one is listening.

My goals for the night include only this:
make the most delicious personal pizza pies
on the whole planet. "Time to get to work!"

Homemade

"If it ain't homemade," Mamaw starts most sentences,
"then it ain't worth eating."
She makes a show of pulling the advertisements
for other pizza spots out of the drawer.
I'm almost 100 percent positive she keeps them there
for this reason alone.

"Giovanni's Pizzeria? Sauce is overly salty. Crust is so-so."

"Flavors of Florence? Tomatoes are not fresh
& the dough is frozen. You can tell. *I can tell.*"

She goes through three more that way,
naming all the chain pizza spots
& the ones two or three towns away,
having tasted all of them
& sharing in detail
why none of 'em
are as tasty
as homemade.

"Anything you make
with your own two hands
is worth it." She smiles
while handing out aprons
& laying out ingredients.

The Kitchen Erupts

Olives & jalapeños, roasted tomatoes,
mushrooms & mozzarella, pineapple & pecorino,
fontina & feta, ham, salami & pepperoni, Parmesan,
paper-thin slices of onion, red peppers & oregano,
olive oil & balsamic, basil & pesto, Italian sausages
& our mouths are watering in no time.

Mamaw does absolutely nothing halfway. Preheats
the oven, puts another record to spinning & dances
while she pulls dough from the fridge & teaches us
how to roll out the perfect pizza pie.

Says, "Dough is simple."

Flour
Salt
Sugar
Olive oil
Love & let it rise.

"Making something from nothing is simple.
Flatten and shape. Stretch and smooth.
Relax and roll. Go easy. Be gentle with it.
Speak to it. Sing to it. Tell it all your secrets.
Watch it take shape. Nourish you. Feed you."

Mariella, StaceyAnn & I eat it up. Both the pizza
& Mamaw's sayings. We load our pies to the max
& stuff our faces 'til we're silly. Wash it down
with Mamaw's sweet & spicy iced tea.
There's enough caffeine to keep us up all night,
& I can't help but be thankful for feeling so full.

After Dinner

We stay awake rambling, playing
rounds of cards, old board games.
The nights always move too fast
when we're together, new dances,
lip-synching songs, telling stories.

"So there I am," StaceyAnn starts,
"about to go down the hill on Waverly,
seeing if I can beat my best time,
when Lucas and Rodney show up
and you-know-who wants to race."

"He's the worst," Mariella says,
all of us knowing she means Lucas,
who makes fun of everyone & everything.
He's all the time trying to finish first
or beat someone at something
or make some kind of scene.

"The worst," StaceyAnn adds.

"You still mean Lucas, right? Not Rodney.
Rodney's still cool and nice, right?" I ask,
trying not to let it show that even the mention
of Rodney's name sends me
into complete panic mode.

"Oh yeah, Rodney's the best.
Not sure why he hangs with Lucas,
but anyway, I beat 'em both so bad
that I swear my tires were smoking.
You know I know my own hill
and my own speed," she adds,
moving in to high-five us both.
"After that, we all rode around together
talking about seventh grade.
Guess they're kinda excited."

"Wonder if they're nervous too?" Mariella asks
no one in particular.

"Definitely not as nervous as me," I say.
"I don't think anyone is as nervous as me."

In the Mirror

While we're all getting ready for bed, we stand together
in front of my tiny bathroom mirror. Toothbrushes out.
I look up & see our reflections. All of us still growing up.

Me

Still so skinny, I nearly disappear. Mamaw says *slim*
but I still wear clothes in the kid section. Childlike
is how I feel. Face full of zits suddenly. My hair
wild & unruly. I want to be sophisticated. Almost
thirteen. My breasts (Mamaw makes me use the correct
word for the correct anatomy) do not exist. My shape
does not exist. Tan now, but by November I'll be
ghostlike. How long until I look the way I'm supposed to?
Even though I'm not totally sure what that means.

Mariella

Head full of thick black hair that tumbles
every which way. She says it can't be tamed,
while wrestling it into a hair tie. Her ponytails
last forever & she's always wishing it shorter
or curlier or easier to manage.
Her brown skin is zit-less. Smooth & acne free
& she's always saying: *Just lucky I guess* since none of us
use any fancy face wash or special lotion.
Mariella isn't even five feet & complains

that she could still use a step stool at the sink.
Mamaw calls her "petite" & high fives her
when the two of them can't reach the top of the cabinet
but I know Mariella wishes
to be taller & wishes for a reason to wear a bra
& all of this makes us the same
as we read magazines that promise bodies
we still don't have.

StaceyAnn

Just shaved half of her head. We all said *WHOA!*
Are you serious!? She was. Easily the gutsiest one of us,
with three earrings up one ear & four up the other.
Seriously, she is not afraid of one thing. Calls herself
"tough" & "strong" & "thick." *Bras are an evil invention,*
she says & prefers long T-shirts & sports bras.
She doesn't care to be any size other than her own.
Olive-toned skin she loves, she calls herself "sun-kissed."
But she'd like bigger biceps
& her calf muscles to be stronger, more defined.
Says she can do twenty-five push-ups in a row
& wants to make it to fifty. We all want something
we don't have. That's kind of comforting to me.

When I Can't Sleep

My nerves stay stuck in my throat.
Eyes opened wide, moonlight slipping
through the window. It's too bright.
I'm too scared. I'm too nervous.
I'm too shy around boys.
What if I say the wrong thing?
Why do I care so much
about what everyone thinks?
Just breathe, relax.

Mamaw says to envision what I want,
so I force my eyes closed.
See Rodney Murphy (who is easily
the most comic-book-obsessed
& funniest kid in our class)
riding his bike
right in my direction.
Imagine the words coming easy & loose.
See myself as relaxed as StaceyAnn
gliding wild down the hill.
Being as free as I am with the people I love.
Talking about designing our own superheroes
& debating about Marvel vs. DC & which universe
is our favorite. Saying something like,
"The best universe is the one you're in,"

& sounding amazing & not too awkward
& not too clunky. But just exactly right.
Cracking jokes & laughing 'til my sides ache,
not so worried about how I'll show up,
just showing up.

See myself confident. Not all caught up
in pretending to be anyone I'm not.

Midnight

I wake up on the couch hours later,
see StaceyAnn sprawled on the floor
& Mariella curled in the couch corner,
all of us snug with blankets & pillows.

The light in the kitchen flashes on,
& I hear Mom making loud sighs
while loading the dishwasher, clanging
pots & pans, opening & shutting the fridge.

"You and your mamaw are one and the same,"
she says, eyeing me. "A mess from here
to the county line." She shakes her head,
gets her eyes to roll all the way around.

"Sorry," I whisper, "it's our fault. We fell
fast asleep. Pizza was great though. Sorry,"
I say again. Start covering bowls, wiping
counters & stealing leftover bites of pie.

"You two make all the mayhem, and I'm left
cleaning it up. It's not fair, Beatrice."
I know she's right. The two of us storm
& clutter, create chaos together.

It's true: most of the time Mamaw makes
the most magnificent of messes & Mom
follows along behind her, cleaning them up.
Mamaw says they're yin & yang.

Interconnected opposites. Slow & fast.
Positive & negative. Quiet & loud. Morning
& night. Summer & winter. Sun & moon.
Earth & sky. Hot & cold. Night & day.

Most of the time, opposites
do not attract, & I'm always in between.
The thread that connects the two, always
a push & pull from here to there.

After Midnight

Mamaw sounds like a train snoring in her room,
asleep in her puffy recliner, book wide open,
sprawled across her chest, lifting up & down.

I cover her with another quilt, study
her silver hair sprouting out, framing
her face like a halo or mane. Wrinkles
etched around her eyes from smiling
& laughing all the time. Crying too.

Mamaw has already lived life
to the fullest. I give her
a silent thank-you
for making me
a little wild
too.

Rise & Keep Shining

That's my mom's favorite saying.
She calls our names & I smell bacon.

"You're cooking?!" I ask, surprised.

"Your mamaw is not the only one
who knows her way around the kitchen,"
my mom says, nearly burning her hand
as she cracks an egg into the skillet.

Mariella & StaceyAnn trail behind me,
taking seats around the table. They both
give me a look when they see my mom
behind the stove. This is a sight to see.

Mamaw is the kitchen wizard, knife wielder,
garden grower, stove chanter, apron wearer.
Mom is the caregiver, nurse-you-well woman,
Band-Aids for your cuts, thermometer
in the middle of the night. Tuck your sheets,
take your pain away.
They have separate skills,
& when one tries to do what the other does best,
there are problems.

"What in the world?" Mamaw asks, wheeling in
& taking the spatula from Mom's hands.
"Lisa, you go on now & relax. I got this."
She nudges my mom with her hip, shoos her away.

"Well, we wouldn't even be able to cook in here
if I hadn't cleaned up after you all last night,"
my mom says, an edge in her voice I hardly ever hear.
We exchange looks, not sure if an argument
is about to break out. "Bea, could you please
give me some space?"

Both Mamaw & I look up. My namesake.
We both know she's talking to Mamaw,
but all of us head on out to the porch,
since it seems like distance
is something we need most.

Beatrice

Maybe my parents
could have chosen a name
not like a granny.

Less grandma, more teenage.
Less arthritic, more athletic.
Less geriatric, more youngish.
Less old-folks home, more spring break.
Less ancient, more modern.
You get the idea.

The fact that it really *is* my mamaw's name
doesn't make it any better.
Fact is—it makes it worse.
Because I love my mamaw
more than the ocean
or french toast
or sleeping in
or bacon.

& when I don't spend all my time hating it,
my name becomes a beacon.
Some light to hang on to
when it's too dark
to see myself.

Porch Swinging

That's where I find Mom late afternoon,
her feet curled up beneath her,
a magazine laid out on her lap.

After the burned bacon & runny eggs,
after the tension & tight talking,
after Mariella & StaceyAnn headed home,
after I tried to ride out the whole afternoon
buried in a book in my room,
after I cleaned the whole kitchen myself,
since Mom & Mamaw headed out
in different directions,
I found myself
feeling more
alone.

"I'm sorry," I say again, taking a seat
swinging right along beside her.
"She's sorry too," I add,
knowing Mamaw hasn't thought twice
about Mom or the kitchen or the mess.
Mom gives me a hard stare.

We both look up.
Mamaw is humming in the garden,

spending time in her sacred space.
Not one care at all.

"Deep down. She's sorry waaayyy
deep down." We both laugh.

"I know your mamaw prides herself
on being unique, a character, just exactly
who she is every second of every day,
but some of the time those eccentricities
make other people feel . . . covered up . . .
like I'm in her shadow," Mom says,
her eyes welling up.
"I love, love that you two are so close,
but sometimes I feel left out."

"I love you," I say to my mom & mean it.
"There's only one Mom and there's only one Mamaw."

We look again & see Mamaw rolling her hips,
dancing to the music of the flowers & cornstalks
twirling in the breeze.

"Thank goodness," Mom says, & we both giggle
knowing this love & this Mamaw
are as rare as they come.

More to Know

"Look at me," Mamaw says later that night.
Both of us back in the kitchen. This time, cleaning
as we go. Mamaw schooling me like always.

"I didn't go to college, barely even finished high school,
all truth be told. Back then, they called it 'country smarts.'
My daddy taught me planting and seeding and seeing
and canning. My papaw & mamaw taught me history
and land and growing and how to tend to the land
and my own hunger. How to manage a kitchen.
That's exactly what I'm teaching to you. Then I learned
how to serve, wait tables, wait on people, learned
to know just exactly what they wanted and needed.
'Course I wanted more for myself," she says. Quieter now.

"Chef. Master gardener. Own a restaurant. Travel
the world." Her eyes mist up. I can tell because she stands
& starts to roll her shoulders back.

"Everything I learned, I learned from the sidelines.
So I've always wanted you to be on the field.
Not learning from some junky old computer
or stuck on a phone. But in it."

Swimming
Jumping

Running
Riding
Flying
Floating
Free.

"That's what I wanted. For both you and me."

Pastry Chef

That's the official name for what Mamaw is.
But seeing as she never went to culinary school
& learned most everything from experimenting,
trying new things, taste testing & searching,
they just call her Ms. Bea at Bardstown Baked,
the delicious dessert shop where Mamaw
has remained queen of cakes & caramels,
ruler of treats & sweets. She's only part-time now,
but in her heyday, she was Queen Bea,
developing new visions,
meringues & candy coatings, fruit pies
& fun flavored ice creams like Kentucky Derby pie swirl
& mint julep sorbet. The owners still love her every idea.
She calls herself a confectionary consultant
& I love that she spends her days inventing new ways
to make people silly with sugary highs.

Mamaw, Mom & Me

Is the way it's been since I was born.
On account of the fact that my dad died
while Mom was seven months along.
On account of slick roads December
riding windy Old Bardstown Road home.
On account of another car spinning still
sliding reckless & relentless toward him.
On account of it being early morning—home
from his night shift at the factory.
On account of new work for a new baby,
on account of that new baby being me.

Things My Dad Was Gonna Be Great At

Football, even though Mamaw says
"It makes your brain blow up
and no one in their right mind
needs to be tackling or getting tackled."
Still, he was good at it.

Medicine, since he always got all A's in science class.
"He sure was a genius," Mamaw says.

Cooking. He could scramble the meanest eggs
this side of the Appalachians. Bake biscuits,
salmon croquettes & garlicky cheese grits.

Crossword puzzles. He got that from Mamaw,
who can do them in high-speed record time.
She says he got most of his greatness
from her. And some (a little) from Papaw,
who she misses most times too.
All the men in our life gone too soon.

She says my dad woulda been great
at everything but that most of all,
he would've been great
at loving me.

Things I'm Gonna Be Great At

Speaking my whole mind.
As Mamaw says,
"Beatrice, honey,
you've got a whole lot to say
and all the words to say it."

Bringing people together.
I've always loved an open house.
Learned that from Mamaw
& the way she keeps our front door
swinging open.

Healing. Learned that from Mom,
who can stitch a wound
& bandage a broken bone
or heart or soul.

Planting. Since Mamaw says
I inherited her green thumb
& can plant any ol' thing
& have the patience
to watch it grow.

Bardstown, Kentucky

Rolling hills, grass
so blue, it's green.
Creek beds
& catching crawdads,
firefly Friday nights.
Fish fry & corn bread.
Fried chicken livers,
pork chops covered
in BBQ. Porch sitting
all day. Glider
or swing, back
& forth. Main Street
slow drawl, honey
pecans, fresh peaches
in the summertime,
a watermelon sliced
straight through.
Voted most beautiful
small town
in Kentucky.
& I for one
believe
every
word.

What Other People See vs. What I See

To other people,
Kentucky
> = country
> = hillbilly
> = backwoods
> = uneducated
> = misunderstood

But to me,
Kentucky
> = home
> = family
> = a garden in bloom
> = everyone who matters
> = my whole life story

They see empty roads
where I see rolling hills.

They see small towns
where I see everyone I know
& who knows me too.

They see small minds
where I see big ol' hearts
& brilliance.

On the news, I hear "poverty"
& "underprivileged." But in my home,
I see a table full of fresh food
from our garden & beds made
with quilts from my great-
great-granny's two hands.

To me, a Kentucky sky is full
of stars & shine. Smells of woods
& fresh earth. Thankful
the people who've raised me up
have taught me to love
where I'm from.

Countryfolk

Mamaw says people all the time
underestimate the South. Think
we're rowdy, unruly & messy,
backward, dirty & unkempt.
Think we don't know nothing.
Imagine us barefoot, dirt roads,
stupid, uneducated, the opposite
of sophisticated. Can't invite us
anywhere.

She laughs in downward dog.
Her long silver strands trailing behind.
Mixes her homemade kombucha
& cracks the spine of her newest
cookbook. Open to sourdough bread
braided in twisted wheat goodness.

"I might be country, but I'm worldly
too," she says, pointing at our map
rising up like a wave behind her.
"Even if I haven't traveled the globe,
I've been there in my books & newspapers
and stories and tall tales. Tell it. I've known

this whole wide world better than most.
And I sure know not to poke fun at someone
for the way they drawl. Where they lay
their head. Or the soil they plant their dreams in."

Not to Brag

Mamaw says, "But our garden
is easily the biggest on the block."

Chock-full of beans, beets,
& bok choy. Cabbage, carrots,

corn reaching up to the clouds.
Cucumber & dill. Summer

squash & swiss chard. Sage,
hot peppers & potatoes.

Arugula we dress homemade
olive oil with lemon & salt.

The sweetest of all sweet
potatoes. Tomatoes, turnips

& thyme. Okra, onion, enough
for dashes of oregano. Meals

are made hearty here. Sprouting wide, weathering & water-

ing. The two of us with the green-
est of thumbs. Watch it all grow.

Getting Old Is Hell

Mamaw says & giggles into her gloves—
full of dirt & holding one earthworm
slimy & still alive in her fingers.
"Creaky bones and all.
You gotta hold on to something,
anything to even get on up.
Your knees give,
your hips ache.
Your body sinks.
I used to be five foot seven, you know?"
She's been lying about that forever.
& everyone knows she's never ever
been taller than five foot four.
"And don't get me started on how hard it is
to keep my mind fresh. Woooo, cobwebs
for days up there. Can't remember one
little thing."
She goes back to digging,
shaking her head just a little.
Jogging memory.
"I wish I was older," I say.
She pops her good hip out & tilts her head.
"Oh, sweet Beatrice. You have plenty of time."
"But I want it now," I say—careful not to whine.
"Wanna be adult now and grown
and know it all."

At this she really starts in,
guffawing & choking on her laughter.
"You think I know it all? Just 'cause you get older
doesn't mean you get smarter. Just means
you ask more questions." I sigh.
Study the day, Mamaw's small body
curled toward me.
I have so many questions myself,
it feels like I'll never know any of the answers.
"I guess I just wish I could predict the future.
See if it's all gonna work out for me.
In the end, you know?"
& as soon as I say it, I see Mamaw's old hurt.
My dad's passing away too soon.
& I see how she imagined a future
that never even made it home that night.
& we both hold each other a little longer.
Somehow find a way to be satisfied with today
knowing no tomorrow is ever promised.

Growing

Mamaw says this is the season,
for germinating & burgeoning.
Big words I have to look up
in the dictionary. Because
we are also the only family
on the block who still owns one.
& our ancient, olden-times
computer takes eons
to come alive. "Books last
longer. They're better," Mamaw
says. I go on & sigh a long one.
Look them up just the same.

Germinate & Burgeon

To germinate is to shoot forth
straight up from the ground.

Rise into existence. Exist. Begin.
Develop from seed or spore.

From bulb to plant. From kid
to girl to young woman. Develop.

To burgeon is to bud. Quick
with flourish. Sprout & arrive.

Too bad I don't feel like either
of those words. Still growing.

Still trying to figure out how to
take up space & show off.

Instead, I'm still somewhere
underground. Beneath it all.

Watching everyone else push up
& grow. Rising high all around me.

How I'd love to be: Beatrice Miller,
queen of the amplify. Expansion even.

Tell Mamaw to watch out for me
& my reckless blossoming.

Night Shift

Mom works from seven p.m. to five a.m.
at Flaget Memorial
& says nursing's the best thing
that ever happened to her.
Acute care & attention, constant contact
& emotional support staff.
Her routine is a roaming rotation
of temperatures, blood work,
maintaining peace & ease.
She supplies what you need
to recover & mend.
Lisa Miller: the human comforter,
maven of meditation & healing.
Mom makes magic out of medicine.
& even though it seems like the whole town
survives & thrives with her help & heart,
sometimes in the middle of the night,
I wish she were using her skills
to make my restlessness go calm.

What I Need from You

Is what my mom has been saying all summer.

"Beatrice Miller,
what I need from you
is your focus and attention.
Your mamaw is getting older
and wilder and messier
and just all over the place."

"This is what I need from you:
laundry washed, folded, and put away
dishwasher loaded and running
counters wiped down
trash taken out
beds made
floors cleared
art supplies put away
dolls and books stored up
your desk organized
your closet organized
your bathroom organized
everything organized
you get the idea
right?"

Sometimes my mom
gets in monologue mode
& talks & talks & lectures
& gives rambling speeches
about our home & the state
of our living situation
& the world. & her voice
is a monotonous ringing
that lasts forever.

What I want to say is:
"I get it! Enough!
Stop talking! It's your house!
You clean!"

But what I say is:
"Yes, ma'am. I'll do better.
I'll help out around the house
and make sure Mamaw is okay.
I promise."

Part Mamaw & Part Mom

Is the way I've always been.

Like Mom, I can hide away
from the world with a book
or journal. Get quiet as can be.

But like Mamaw, I can fire up,
get to dancing & singing,
flinging my emotions around.

I go from solo to crowd
easy as can be. From calm
to rowdy. From low to high.

The great copycat. Play it up
or down. Depending on who
I'm with, what's expected of me.

From still to nonstop. Sometimes
I'm so busy trying to mimic them
that I forget to just be me.

Summer Still

& we ride our bikes for hours.
Bright orange for me. Purple dream
for StaceyAnn & fiery red for Mariella.
We all bought them at the same time. Saved
up from two months of babysitting. Jackpot
as we coast to Rincón Mexicano, the best
spot in town since Mariella's folks
opened it three years ago. Her mom
waves us in for chips & guacamole. We tell
the tallest tales when we're together. Laugh
with our mouths wide open. StaceyAnn says this year,
we'll rule the school. Even that doesn't sound
cool. But we agree. Dunk more chips, drink—
rounds of Sprite arrive. It's still summer,
still warm enough to imagine she's right.

Wanna Catch Crawdads?

Mariella asks. She's leaned on her bicycle,
the sun a fat glow on her face.
"We could work on our tree house too?
We still got a little more to do
to make it our perfect secret hideout.
& look, I got my *abuelo*'s tool belt."
Perfection.

& I barely get my goodbye out, running
full speed to race alongside her bike.
StaceyAnn meets us at the corner, her arms
loaded up with chocolate chip cookies
& Ale-8-1 Limited Edition Orange Cream.

"Yes!" we all shout, tumbling over one another
toward the creek bed. Only takes ten minutes
to ride outta the neighborhood & straight
to our hidden spot—where we can just be
quiet & unknown to all the adults in our lives.
It's the place I love best, away from it all.

Cutoff jean shorts & raggedy T-shirts:
we're wearing the perfect summer uniforms.
Flip-flops, feet free & an old upside-down sled
to keep the critters in while we study 'em.

Been spending end-of-August days like this.
Pounding nails & boards to the side
of our favorite tree, just far enough away
so no one can bother us, no one can interrupt.
We've hammered in bookshelves & made room
for all the things we collect along the way.
A hammock high above the bluegrass to sit
& watch the day.

"Tastes just like a Dreamsicle," StaceyAnn says,
popping the tops & handing out a round.
"Small batch, seasonal flavor," she reads.
To me it tastes just like summer.
& sugar, of course. All the sweetest things
about hoping something lasts forever.

Tree House Where I Hold My Dreams

Long after Mariella & StaceyAnn ride away,
I find myself getting comfortable. Relaxing.
Pull my diary & pen out, start to swing
in our perfectly positioned hammock
that stretches between two tree limbs
& lean my head all the way back.
Try to hold on to this feeling.

"Anything you make
with your own two hands
is worth it," Mamaw is always saying.

This afternoon, I think she's right
as I take in our work. The fabric
we've wrapped & draped,
the trinkets we've placed
in secret parts of our tree.
Small crystals, old dolls & toys,
parts of our lives we don't play with anymore
but don't want to forget either.

This space, all our own.
StaceyAnn nailed in an old mirror
to create a kaleidoscope with the sun.
I look right into it—see my reflection

& all the parts that make me who I am
or who I am supposed to be.
Worthy & whole
trust all the parts
put it all together.
Want to make myself shining
and worth it
too.

City Pool

StaceyAnn can do the best backstroke
while Mariella can somersault twice
atop the high dive. I'm awesome
at inhaling loads of nachos with extra
cheese & floating into the abyss. Oblivion.
Beneath all that chlorine, I'm part
mermaid—all flowing & beautiful, part
still me. The parts I still like. Strong
arms & legs. My feet for pushing through.
Underwater, I'm sea creature & girl still
imaginary & real at the same time.

Swim Team Girls

Besides showing off & eating until we're silly,
the three of us + Zoey Samuels
(who is eleven but acts seventeen)
make up the Bardstown Barracudas relay team
representing the best public pool in the whole county.
Practice happens three days a week
& we hustle into the cool pool
swimming lap after lap.

Whistle blows
Dive
Freestyle
Submerge
Practice
Race
Paddle
Butterfly
Free
Back

Whistle blows
Rest
Float
Glide
Wade

Dip
Crawl
Slide
Wash
Drift

Our final meet of the summer is coming up.
Coach Crane tells us to sleep hard, hydrate
& eat full meals to keep ourselves afloat.

I've Been Thinking

about what "staying afloat"
really means. Above water. With all your breath.
Wondering how to stay unsinkable when school starts.
Not be taken down by feeling left out,
not pretty or smart or grown or mature enough.
Pulled between wanting to stay a kid
but ready to be a teenager. Looking in the mirror
& loving what I'm seeing. Being as fast & strong
& smart as my mom & mamaw say I am.
Believing it myself.

How to be weightless when everything feels so heavy.

Race Day

We stretch our arms to the sky,
run in place. Jumping jacks.
Mariella kickboards across the pool.
StaceyAnn plunges below sound.

We're up against our biggest rivals:
Washington County Wave Runners.
Even their name makes zero sense.
A wave runner is a vehicle—a watercraft.
It's not a fish. It's motorized. Fake fast.
Besides they're from some fancy
country club that none of us
care a lick about. We gotta beat 'em.

Meanwhile, a barracuda is fearsome
& ferocious. We read all about it.
Designed shirts & hats. Large
& predatory. That's what we are.

What I'm thinking is:

Can't touch us.
Lightning below water.
Watch out.
Unstoppable.

Medley Relay

We get ready. StaceyAnn is first
because her backstroke is fastest.
She starts in the water. Goggles on.
Fiery & fierce. Mariella next. Flying
with her breaststroke. Pushing through.
Zoey is our butterflyer. Her limbs
leaping through the water. I'm the anchor.
Waiting at the other end to be tagged.
Always have been. Always will be.
Coach says I'm the best freestyler,
& I take the compliment.

Nerves are popping in all directions.
Heart moving double-time. Breath short.

The Wave Runners look tough & speedy.
Giving us side-eyes, hands on their hips.
They are not scared of us. That is certain.

The Whistle Blows

We're off!
StaceyAnn plunges back.
Her arms a riptide.
We holler.
"Go, go, go!"
Jumping up & down.
Following her ripple
making the pool an ocean.
She tags the side.
Mariella dives up, then under,
up, breath, stroke;
she's all fish tonight.
"We're beating them!" I shout.
Zoey swoops in after.
Her shoulders small but powerful,
breaking the surface.
I can see we're in the lead.
Shake my stress.
Close my eyes.
Thankful for this.
A second of breathing,
when Zoey hits the side,
I burst through.
My arms a wild charge.

I can hear Mom & Mamaw
cheering me on.
Mamaw's whistle
rings through the crowd,
& Mom yells:
"Goooooo, Beatrice, goooooo!"
So I do.
Uncontrollable.
Unstoppable.
Just exactly
like I imagined.

We Win

"Yeah, yeah, yeah," StaceyAnn shouts,
perfecting her favorite dance moves on the sideline.
I know it's not nice to brag,
but I can't help it as I whoop & holler right alongside.
Mariella & I go in for our handshake.
High-five, turn around, dip low, shake,
twirl around, spin, slide, bring it back.
StaceyAnn tackles us so that we all tumble
splashing into the deep end of the pool.
Coach tells us we're up for the ribbon ceremony,
so we stand together. All of us still soaked.
Our hometown crowd cheers
while they crown us county champions
& hand out smooth, shiny ribbons
with #1 printed in shimmering gold.

Dinner on Us

Mariella's folks announce.
We dry off, hit the locker room to change
& all end up on the picnic tables at the playground.
Outside the city pool, the sky is just starting
to go dark.

Mariella, StaceyAnn, Zoey & I share a table,
the sun still lasting on our skin.

My mom & mamaw sit at a table with the grown folks.
Mariella's mom pulls out all our favorites:
chips & their homemade salsa with jalapeños
& roasted tomatoes. Corn on the cob wrapped in foil
with mayonnaise, cayenne & cotija cheese.
Handmade tortillas with pork carnitas.
Mamaw pulls bottles of Coca-Cola from her small cooler
& a jar of her special Kentucky Benedictine Dip
loaded with garden cucumbers, onion, sour cream,
cream cheese & cayenne too. It's a Southern standby
that she spreads on a few tacos.
She calls it "country-fied Mexican" & everyone tries it.
I love the way we all mix & blend cultures & flavors.

StaceyAnn's dad plays music from the back of his truck,
& we stand on top of the monkey bars, swing

until we're silly, push each other on the merry-go-round,
& laugh & laugh, replaying our star turns
underneath the water.

As the sun finally dips into the earth,
we start to howl & shriek,
giddy on the sugar & caffeine,
still on a winner's high.

At the Playground

We all pile our legs together as we spin
on the merry-go-round.
Zoey gasps when she sees my legs.
"Okay, seriously, Beatrice, *your legs*
look just like Dotty, *my schnauzer.*
"Wow," she says again, eyeing them close.
"What?" I ask, looking down at my legs
& comparing them to StaceyAnn's & Mariella's.
StaceyAnn doesn't shave, but her hair is baby fine,
but Mariella does (did? when?), since her legs
are silky smooth.
"Shut up," StaceyAnn says.
"But they're soooo hairy!" Zoey says again.
(Reminder: Zoey is eleven . . .
but she might as well be seventeen.
The way she acts & talks—is just plain teenage.)
"Besides, if you shave your legs, you swim faster,"
she says, running a hand along her own.
What? I am thinking. *An eleven-year-old shaves her legs
& I'm stuck looking like a beast. Whyyyyy?!*
StaceyAnn says, "That's not true, 'cause Beatrice
is the fastest swimmer on our team.
Besides, no one cares if you shave your legs or not."
"They will when you get to school," Zoey says.
"My older sister says: the hairier the legs,

the weirder the kid." She starts to laugh wicked
& we know she's joking, but I can't help but feel
like she might be right.

Seriously

"Don't listen to her," StaceyAnn says
as Zoey gives us all air-kisses
& heads home with her family.
"She's just a kid."

"That's how I feel," I say,
embarrassed, looking at my hairy legs.
"I haven't even started my period,"
I whisper as the merry-go-round
starts to slow all the way down.

"Don't worry—it's definitely
not a big deal," Mariella says.

"That's because you already got yours,
and I don't even need to wear a bra,"
I say, leaning back & looking at the sky,
the stars exploding all above me.

"That sucks too," StaceyAnn says.
"Just be thankful
you don't have to think about it yet."

And I know, they're trying their best
to just make me feel better. Enough.

But when Mariella kicks the ground
to pick up the pace, I feel like they're moving
at lightning speed. And I'm just trying
to hold on.

Time to Go

Mom announces when it's clear she's had enough
of our wildness. "It's getting late. Time to head home."

"Lisa, come on, give 'em a little more time.
It's not every day four young women are crowned
county champions," Mamaw shouts,
& the three of us get to howling,
sounding just like wolves in the night.

"Please, Mom, just ten more minutes?" I beg.

Mom gives me *The Look*.
The one that says:
Enough
I'm tired
You're pushing it
It's time to go
Don't make me lose my temper.

It's amazing all the things my mom can say
with just one look.
"Besides, you girls need to start getting ready for school,
going to bed earlier. Come on now."

"Oh, Lisa, come on. Live a little," Mamaw says,
& I can see she's already pushing it too far.

"It's time," my mom says, & we know she means
business.

Mamaw and I let out long sighs, give hugs all around,
& pile into the car.

"Could you two get in my court at least once
this summer? Please,"
my mom says, eyeing Mamaw and me.

"I just want you to have a little fun," Mamaw says.
"Let your hair down. Take it easy."

"I am having plenty of fun. All the fun. The most fun,"
my mom says, clearly not having any fun at all.

She turns the radio on
& all we hear is static.

At Home

Mom & Mamaw get into it on the porch.
They tell me to shower all that chlorine off,
but I wait & listen outside the door.
The benefit of our house being so old & so small
is that you can hear everything if you try hard enough.

"Bea, I need you to get behind me on my decisions.
I feel like I'm always the bad one, & I can't live like this."

"Lisa, I hear you. I do, but you gotta go easy on her.
She's a great kid—the best. You've gotta let her stay a kid
for as long as possible."

"She's about to be in the seventh grade, Bea.
She's not a kid anymore. She's a young woman.
She needs to start acting like it. Grow up a little.
Stop acting so wild."

There is a pause and a silence so long, it seems like
they might know I'm steady listening.

But then I hear Mamaw's voice ask this question:
"Why would you want her to stop being so free?"

The Bathroom Mirror

That night, right before I shower,
I take all my clothes off & stand
steady & strong. Look at myself
in front of the full-length mirror.
Flat as a board. Thin. Too skinny.
Beanpole. Would all describe me.
Fluffy hair. Not tall enough. Not
curvy enough. Not woman enough.
Too hairy. Too awkward. Too out
of place. Too out of this world.
Too wild. Too babyish. Too kid-like.
I let out a quiet howl. Turn around,
look from side to side. Try to love
all of me the way I am.

When I Can't Sleep

I rummage through my mind.
Want to know the way other eyes
will see me. If they will think
I am enough. Just on my own.
& because it's late enough
& dark enough
& quiet enough
& I'm alone enough,
I get to thinking
what summer has been like
for the boys in my class,
the ones I like,
the ones who are funny
& silly
& goofy.
& the ones I don't like,
the ones who are rude
& mean
& annoying.
Mostly, I am thinking of Rodney again,
who sat beside me in homeroom last year
& told me he wished he could be a superhero
when he grows up.
Of course, he was kidding,
but deep down

I wish I could be one too.
& I wonder most of all
if superpowers exist
& if they do,
what ours will be
when seventh grade begins.

Sunburn Sunday

"It's high time we take the kayak out,"
Mamaw says as soon as I wake up.
"Kentucky rivers are a surefire way
to get your brain straight."

We pack up the car together & drive.
Mom says she has to catch up at home,
but I think she just wants a break from us.

Mamaw rolls all our windows down
& plays the Carolina Chocolate Drops.
Turns the volume up all the way
until we reach the water.

"Sometimes you gotta trade chlorine
for fresh water. Clears the head," she says.

Paddle
Paddle, paddle
Paddle, paddle, paddle
Paddle, paddle, paddle, paddle.
Breathe nature, air, water
& what lives below the surface.
Wake earlier, work harder, care
for it, nurture & navigate how to love.

Mamaw says swimming in the river
can take all your cares away.
& jackknifing straight down to the bottom
was all they got round to doing in the summer
when they were kids. All snakes & crawdads.

Mom thinks rivers are filthy & says so.
She was a city kid. Grew up fast
in big-time Louisville. She thinks diseases
& snakebites are more likely what I'll find,
& part of me thinks she's right. Mud caked
between my toes & murky clouds below.

But more of me wants to take the risk. Dive
beyond the shallow. Go deep & submerge.
Mamaw says I've got to become one
with the water. Grow a tail & fins.
Become part fish. Pretend to know
exactly what I'm doing.

Out on the Water

Surrounded by sky,
so much of life feels
possible. Like anything
could happen at any moment.

I am who I am because of
river water & trout, air & sunshine.

We kayak from one end
of the river to the other
& land on the shallow shore.

Mamaw calls the orders:
"Switch, dig deep, switch,
dig deeper." We sun bake
& lay our paddles aside.

Let the breeze buoy us.
It's the end of a summer
I wish could last forever.

Sometimes I feel like
I should be running
all the races
doing all the things

hurry up & get there
go ahead & get my life started
& shave my legs
& get a boyfriend
& get boobs
& feel pretty enough
feel enough
enough
that I'll stop wanting
so much of the time.

& sometimes I just feel
like now. Like still. No
wind & rush or beat
the clock. Just exactly
right where I need to be.

When Mamaw says, "Slow
it all the way down,"
finally I do. Take a big
gulp of breath. & let it
all
out.

Mamaw's Lifestyle

"Is lean, mean & clean," she always says,
bucking trends of nicotine from her days
& of course alcohol & e-cigarettes & any ol'
substance that can change or shift a day
lickety-split. Always says her daddy liked
the liquor best. It being Bardstown and all.
Bourbon Capital of the World. How most
of them men made their money. Distilling
& all. Corn to sour mash to downright drunk.
Says it takes a whole lotta willpower
to stay steady in the right here & now.

And when she says, "I get high on life," & giggles
with her silver-wicked laugh, I kind of believe her.
In a yoga headstand, she shrieks when blood
rushes from tips of her toes to top of her brain
& sings "Hallelujah" when a recipe tastes exactly
the way it promises to. Tongue to taste buds.
Says she saw a whole mess of hurt coming up
& didn't want it re-created in front of me. Life
is finest alert & alive. Don't want your mind
messed with or amplified. Says living right
can be the highest of highs right up to the sky.

Summer for Dinner

I.

Mamaw shouts from the garden, her voice
drifting through my open window. I race

down the stairs, grab her favorite bowl
& send the screen door sailing. Kneeling

together, we gather ears of corn huddled
close inside their husks. Make a mile-high pile.

"Now the tomatoes," she says. Pulling straight
from the vine. They smell of earth & dirt. We

sniff their flavor. Mamaw holds them to her
apron. Like vegetable babies—we pat & caress,

brush the muck from their crimson skins. She
holds the smallest out to me & I take a bite,

the juice rolling down my chin. Savory & sweet
at the exact same time. Can August last forever?

II.

Turn on the stove & get that water boiling. Salt
& one tablespoon of whole milk. Secret recipes

are Mamaw's specialty. But she knows I can keep
them to myself. "Get to slicing," she says. "And table set."

So I wash & cut thick slices of tomatoes. Their juice
staining the counter. Load them on a plate & pepper

& olive oil them up. Waiting for the water to boil,
we grab chairs to shuck the corn. "Speed never wins,"

Mamaw says, so I slow it way down. Smooth away
each sliver of silk sticking to the white & yellow corn.

When the cooking is done & everything
is tender & set out, we slather butter, more salt,

& Mamaw's special cayenne & garlic on top. We
feast until we both feel full from our own backyard.

III.
For dessert, Mamaw pulls the vanilla ice cream
from the fridge. Slices the last of the peaches

& slides them inside our bowls. "Porch swing,"
we say at the same time. & sway medium high,

both our legs kicking the same rhythm. Devour
& tell stories until the sun gets low, low in the sky.

Some Nights

Mariella & StaceyAnn
show up & out. Bring
loads of cheese puffs
& soda. Stash them quiet
in my bedroom, late-
night craving fixes.

Mamaw makes dinner
out of fried okra, rice
so full of salt & butter
that our mouths celebrate,
vegan hot dogs sizzling
on the grill. "It's all about
balance," she says. Grins
before turning in for TV
& her crossword puzzles.

The backyard is ours;
we collect mason jars
with tops, go exploring
to catch fireflies, fast
in our palms, swatting
high fives as they glow
& shine, their wings wide
in our hands. "Look, look!"

we all holler. Name them,
see who can catch the most.

StaceyAnn wins this time,
counting their light; they
glitter through our grip.
Our faces full of sweat,
we laugh while letting go.
Their small bodies
look like fireworks
flying from our fingers.

How I Feel vs. How I'm Supposed to Feel

Inside:
Let's play dolls
Let's play house
Let's play chef
Let's catch crawdads
Let's catch fireflies
Let's pretend
Let's fight crime & fly
through the sky.
Let's write our own stories
& comic-book adventures.
Let's save the day
our own way.
Devour junk food
Sleep all day
TV all night
Play make believe
Ride bikes forever
Ride scooters forever
Roller-skate forever
Walk downtown forever.
Not one care.
Clothes? Don't care
Hairstyle? Don't care
Makeup? Don't care
Fitness? Don't care

Fun? Yes please.
Just be ourselves
Just be us
Just be free
Just be twelve
Not one worry
Not one care.

Outside:
Let's be cool
Let's be smooth
Let's be attitude
Let's be different
Let's be unique.
Obsess about hair
Care about makeup
Running in place
Running around downtown
Obsess over clothes
Be stylish forever
Just be better
Pretend you're perfect
Pretend you're relaxed.
Don't play dolls
Don't play house
Stop playing games
Babies play games
Be almost thirteen.

Mariella Says

Her older sister, Mira,
swears push-ups work
for building pectoral
muscles (her words).
& we believe her
'cause she's going
to med school
when she graduates.
& we all know
what bigger pecs
will mean. So
that's how Mamaw
finds me. Plank
position. & grins.
'Cause she knows
too. "Sweet Beatrice,"
she says, seeing me
already breaking a sweat.
I sigh. Know the truth
when I look at Mamaw,
her small frame. See
my shape in hers.
"It's hard to love
a thing you can't have.
But maybe the truth

is you don't really want
that after all.
Maybe deep down,
you're happy just the way
you're s'posed to be."

Wrong Again

Is what I write in my diary. The truth is:
a bigger bra size is definitely what I want.
No jokes about it. A figure. You know.
One that people talk about. Write notes about.
Put on the cover of magazines.
Wanting What You Can't Have
is the title of my whole middle school life.
& for seventh grade, I want a whole new me.
Let's call it Jackpot: the Beatrice Miller story.
Or: Gold Medal Life.
She got all she was asking for.
& her mamaw was (for once) wrong.
She loved every glorious & awesome minute of it.

Dear Diary,

The other truth is . . . I just want to be noticed,
liked, flirted with even. Want people to think
about me when I'm not around, to miss me,
to want to know more about me. It's true,
I want the girls in my grade to think I'm cooler
than I really am and want some of the boys,
but mostly just Rodney, to think I'm funny & pretty
& want to know more about me. The same way
I want to know everything about him.
I feel different than I did two months ago,
& I want everyone else to see how much I've changed.
Want them to ask questions & be interested
in the answers.

Hopeful,

Beatrice

Questions for Mamaw & Mom

"School starts soon. You know this.
So here are some things I need to know,"
I say, sitting them both down.

"Can I get a cell phone? You should realize
I am almost thirteen, or will be in November.
I need a cell phone. My own digits. Ways
to reach & find me. Desperate. You call,
I answer. Simple. Everyone else has one.
Please?"

"Can I get a new computer? One that works,
one that isn't built for giants. A laptop even?
I'll get better grades; I'll teach you both
how the Internet works. Lead you straight
to the technological future. You can trust me."

"Can I get all new clothes? Seriously?
All my outfits are from Goodwill,
someone else's good time. Me,
I'm stuck in vintage, secondhand.
Can we go to the mall?
A real store?
Anything?"

"And last but not least. Can I wear makeup?
Mascara? Lip balm? Eyeliner? I watched a tutorial.
YouTube showed me the techniques.
They promise I will look fresh
and hip and young. How about
a highlighting stick?
Anything to give me just a little
cover-up. Before I'm completely
exposed in the seventh grade? Help me?
Please?"

Neither of Them Listens

This is what they have in common.
A shared interest in ignoring my wants & needs.
My heart's every desire (I read that in a book).
My heart wants to be connected to the world.
My heart wants to prove I'm getting older.
My heart wants my face to look thirteen.
My heart wants a freakin' personal computer
where I can google to my heart's delight.
My heart wants a cell phone so I can text
Mariella & StaceyAnn heart emojis
when I really, really, really love something.
My heart understands that I will die
if I can't get some privacy & space.

Mamaw Says

"No seventh grader needs a mobile device."
Old-fashioned.
Doesn't even call it a cell phone, God forbid.
"What you need is some strong letter-writing skills,
penmanship, a solid cursive curl to your letter 'B.'
Sharp pencils, smooth pens, sturdy stationary."
Too bad my eyes can't roll into my head,
'cause I roll them so hard, they almost disappear.
Mamaw snaps back. Says, "Don't act so smart;
you young people think you know it all. But you
are just getting started. Brand new in the world."
I sigh. Know I'll never win when she gets going.
She might be old, but she's fast. Quick skilled
& always has an answer to all my arguments.
Most times, I know she's right.

But Lately, I Want

everything I can't have. A crush to crush back;
shiny, smooth hair; no pimples preparing to pop;
the cool girls to invite me to their parties; parties
in general; to have a first kiss that's not awkward
or sloppy or gross. To have a first kiss at all. To start
my period already so I don't have to wait for disaster
or have it be a disaster. But most of all, I want a phone.
Ways to communicate with the outside world. More so,
though, a way to distract myself from all the things
I want but somehow can't seem to have.

What My Mom Can't Afford

The pair of fancy jeans I saw at the mall.
They're so cool, they don't even have a brand name.
Mariella says that's luxury & I agree.

A new computer.
Instead, I'm busy *click-clack*ing
on an old desktop that's as big as Mars
& sits in the hallway for the whole block to see
what I'm looking up.

A new phone. Oh! Any ol' phone at all for that matter.

A new car. It'd be super awesome to not show on up
everywhere in a beat-up ol' brown station wagon.

She can't afford avocados every week.
You know in some places they grow on trees,
but in landlocked Kentucky, they're three dollars a pop.
Yawn is what I think but don't say out loud.

Soda, since she says,
"I'm not paying hard-earned money for your teeth to rot
right out of your sweet little mouth."

She can't afford big family vacations to far-flung
destinations (I read the term "far-flung destination"
in a travel magazine at school & I like the sound of it).
I've never been anywhere.
Never even been on an airplane before.

"Saving for the future," is what she says.
"College or bust," is what she says.
"You wanna travel the world so badly, then you better
get a part-time job or start reading all them books
like Mamaw does."

"New, new, new, new, all you ever want is new,"
my mom says, & it's not that I always want new.
It's just that I'm tired of always trying to pretend
I'm satisfied with old.

Questions for Dad

What were you like when you were twelve
on the way to thirteen? Mamaw says "rowdy,"
"raucous," "renegade" would describe you.
Tells it you were accelerated, raced
your motorbike on country roads, dust
in your tracks. Loved dancing & singing.
Tried anything, tried it twice.

Your voice is an echo
I can sometimes hear in my dreams.

Do you miss me? Do you wish
you could see me? Almost a teenager?
Sometimes I wake after seeing you in my sleep.
Heavy with missing you.
Someone I didn't even know.
Why did you have to leave so soon?

Mamaw says she sees you in me. My drawl,
the wave of my hair. Says I have your smile
& eyes. "Spitting image" is what she says,
holding me to her. If there's a heaven,
& you're up in it, does it ache to watch me
grow up without you? & if there's not one,
then I think of you in Mamaw's garden,

blooming each summer. A peony folding
out over & over—peeling awake beside us
in our own backyard.

Ways to Disappear

Call StaceyAnn.
Call Mariella
from your LANDLINE!
Tell them you are worried
your mom & mamaw
are trying to keep you
a kid forever. Whine
as quietly as possible
in the kitchen, since you
are on a LANDLINE.
Old, clunky phone
connected to the wall
& available for everyone
to witness.

Whisper: *Save me!*
Someone, anyone,
pick me up. Seriously.
Need an exit plan.
A getaway. Drive
in the country? Elizabethtown?
Louisville? Lexington?
Ask one of your reasonable
family members to help me!

Pick me up
& take me
away!

Bluegrass Diner

is the absolute best. & here are the reasons why.

1. It's StaceyAnn's dad's favorite spot. He loves
   the coffee with extra cream & three sugars,
   & if we beg enough, he'll take us on his day off.
   Paradise.
2. Waffles are delicious, especially when they're full
   of pecans & covered in butter & syrup.
   & best of all, Mariella always splits hers with me.
   Perfection.
3. Salty pickles on my egg & cheese sandwich.
   My favorite waitress gives me an extra plateful
   for free.
4. Hash browns loaded with sweet onions
   & drenched in American cheese. Glorious.
5. StaceyAnn puts three pieces of bacon in her grits,
   but the order comes with four.
   Who do you think gets the extra bacon?
   Me. Yes!
6. Everything else. The talking. Laughing.
   Sharing soda & hot chocolate. Sweet & salty.
   Both at once. Sometimes life is so delicious,
   it feels like I can eat & eat & eat & never get full.

Singing Sisters

Sometimes StaceyAnn's dad lets us roll the windows
all the way down & turn the radio all the way up.
His regular job is in construction, but his side jobs
include: musician, carpenter, mechanic & car DJ.
I always imagine him & my dad woulda been the best
of friends. He raises the volume, & we let the sweet-
smelling Kentucky air wrap & curl around us. Our voices
thundering & strong. We throw our arms up, shake
& dance in our seats. We let loose. In the back seat,
Mariella throws her arm around my shoulders, pulls
me in close. StaceyAnn looks behind from the front
& we all laugh, sing so loud that we shake the trees
& hillsides with the sound of our song. Let the whole
dang town & county & state know we're here,
know we exist. & we're ready for the seventh grade.

Period

Not the punctuation.
The real deal.
The menstruation station.
Worst word ever.
My body cramps.
My back aches.
Not ready yet.
Thought I was.
But still scared.
Even more so.
Everything's always changing.
Moving too fast.
School starts soon.
Tampons & pads arrive.
Too much talking.
My brain hurts.
I'm constantly embarrassed.
Too much attention.
My body exists.
And it's awkward.
And also uncomfortable.
I wanted this.
I really did.
I was ready.
Now I'm not.

Can't go back now.
Full speed ahead.
That's what Mamaw says.
Mom starts crying.
Mamaw starts celebrating.
Makes me tea.
Extra honey everything.
Heating pad placed.
Quilt thrown over.
Remote in hand.
Mamaw, Mom, me.
Not so bad.

Mom Says

"Just so you know, now that your period has arrived,"
(as if it's a package I've been waiting for
as opposed to my entrance to womanhood)
"you can get pregnant. You're officially a woman."
"OMG, why would you even say that?" I shout,
surprising myself & Mamaw, who perks up at us.
"I haven't even kissed anyone yet," I hiss-whisper.
Not even close. Not even almost close. Not even
anywhere in the vicinity of close. *Jeez.* Mamaw holds in
a giggle and says, "Everything has its time. You
can never be too careful, Beatrice." "Your body
is your own," we both say in unison. A song I've heard
hundreds of times. 'Course I'd read *Our Bodies, Ourselves*
& *It's Perfectly Normal.* & I knew it was, but ugh, hearing
my mom & mamaw talking about me as if I'm not even here
makes me wish I wasn't. When I retreat to my room, Mom
calls out, "Should we order takeout?" Why can't my family
be normal?

Period Drama

Later that night, I hear my mom crying & laughing
on the phone with her best friend, Cindy, who I call
Aunt Cindy, even though she's not my real, real aunt.
She's telling her about me getting my period.
I'm about to lose it on her when I hear her say,
"Can you believe it? Just when she started hers,
mine is starting to end. Her life is just beginning,
and I'm so happy for her, but . . .
& then there is a silence
as big as the mountains heading out of town.

Rising
      Rising

But what? I want to shout. *Is she mad at me? Hurt, sad?*

"You know, I always thought that I'd have another baby,
somehow give Beatrice a sibling, but every month
that goes by, I just feel older and older and like somehow
I'm not giving her enough."

I resist the urge to yell out, *You give me everything,*
even though I complain, it's enough, you're enough.
My life is complete & enough.
You & Mamaw & this house & my room & my heart,
all of it is here & enough, enough, enough.

"You know, I met someone," my mom says so quietly
that I have to lean on her doorframe, "so I guess all
is not lost." There is a pause, & I almost push her door in.
"Harrison Douglas. Yeah, he's my age. Perfect.
Medical sales. Met him at the hospital.
Can you believe it? Sometimes he shows up early
just to see me before my shift ends.
Also, he's got a great head of hair."
I hear my mom start to laugh, & then she says,
"I haven't told Bea or Beatrice yet. But soon.
I think it's about time. And I really think
it's about time for me to have some
real happiness. A chance
at love."

I Resist the Urge to Yell—

I love you! You love me!
We love each other. & Mamaw too!
We have loads & loads of love.
& real happiness too.

Harrison Douglas?! Who the hell
is Harrison Douglas? & WHY
does he have two last names?!

Google Search: Harrison Douglas

Before she leaves for work, Mom comes in my room.
She wants to congratulate me again. "Your period is here!
I am so happy for you. Rest easy tonight,"
she says before kissing my forehead
& walking out the door for her shift.

As soon as her car is out of the driveway, I rush
to turn the computer on with hopes it will actually
power up by the end of the decade. It chugs along.
I tell Mamaw I have some research to do
before school starts & need technology to do it.
Mamaw hardly ever checks up on me, since she thinks
computers can't hold a candle to the human mind
(her words) & that our particular computer is possessed.
She's not wrong, & she definitely does not believe
in the modern world. At all.

Google Search: Harrison Douglas. Images pop up.
His hair certainly is something to talk about.
It poufs up & off his head. Who in the world . . . ?
As soon as I go for a deeper dive, Mamaw arrives,
a cup of hot jasmine tea steaming in her palms.
"That some new teacher of yours?" I close the tab
fast as possible. "No, no, no, it's . . . I don't even know,"
I lie. Mamaw can tell but says nothing. "I'll do this later,"

I say, closing up the computer, figuring Harrison Douglas
& his hairdo can wait. Besides, they'll probably break up
before I ever even meet him.

'Specially when Mom realizes
she's got us & all the love
in the world
right here.

Gardens, Books & Bourbon

Mamaw's club meets every month at our place.
They take over the kitchen, mixing cocktails
& mocktails. "Old-Lady Brain Trust"
is what Mamaw calls them. Vintage. Veterans
with thousands of stories to tell & hundreds
of years between them. Seven in all. They are
Old Bardstown. Keepers of secrets.
They say, "Beatrice, you look just like your mamaw."
They never say I look like my mom. Believe me.
I've listened real close. & I'd like them to.
Don't get me wrong, Mamaw is striking
with her wild hair & strong jawline. But Mom
is the real stunner, with the smoothest skin,
deep brown eyes, & hair that loops in curls
around her heart-shaped face. She's five foot eleven
& can reach to all the counters, her muscles
perfectly strong & fit. But I'm all Mamaw.
Scrappy & rough around the edges.

"Don't slouch," they say when I start
my daydreaming. "Aren't you sweet.
Be sure to clear your plates. What a doll.
Be sure to keep up at school this year.
Such a good girl. Don't talk back to your elders.
Have another helping. Don't eat too much.
Aren't you smart. Don't correct your mamaw."

Ahhhh, is what I think in my head. Complicated.
They want me quiet & loud. Spunky & timid.
Confident & modest. Bashful & bold. All at once.
Everything at the same time. Say back in the day
that's what was asked of them. I wonder
why they're still asking it of me.

Three Days Before School Starts

Begin the begging for real.

"Hairy legs = ugly.
Smooth legs = pretty.
Smooth + me = cool.
I saw it with my own eyes
twirling on the merry-go-round.
Heard it from Zoey Samuels,
a freakin' fifth grader.
Let me shave my legs.
Please! I can't be caught
looking like a schnauzer!"

"A what?" Mamaw asks,
acting like she's never seen
a hairy dog or my hairy legs
& thought they looked alike.

"I look like a beast," I say.

"Beatrice, don't worry so much
about what everyone else thinks."

"Don't blame me.
Blame middle school.

Blame peer pressure.
Blame razor blades.
Ads targeting girls.
Blame Mariella, StaceyAnn.
Blame their moms.
& their grannies.
& their smooth legs.
Don't blame me.
But seriously, please?
Mamaw? Mom? Anyone?"

Two Days Before School Starts

"Not yet," they both say. "Wait
until the eighth grade," they say.
"It'll just grow thicker. Wait."

Ah, so I can be a pariah, I think.
Run my hands over the fuzz.
Right now, I am part animal.

Bear. Wild boar. My legs like
a fur coat I'm sporting. School
will slaughter me. Gym class
will be the death of me.

Annihilation by laughter. Boys
who can't even grow facial hair
will take their anger out on me.

Busting up about the wooly
mammoth covering ankle to
upper thigh. I'll just about die.

Drama

Is what Mamaw calls me
when she thinks I'm over-the-top.

So instead of lecturing,
she pulls the last cherry tomatoes

from her garden. Slices
them over flatbread with mozzarella

& extra kalamata olives.
The way the two of us always love.

"Love," she says, "is a warm oven
at the deep end of summertime. Love

is not what everyone else
is doing all the time. Being your own self

instead. Love is out of place
& unique. Eccentric sometimes. A standout.

Love doesn't always fit in
& doesn't all the time want to." Pours me

sweet tea for the porch swing,
kicks us slow & steady while we wait.

Love is a constant rocking
& will hold you no matter what it takes.

Gardening with Mamaw

"Just so you know, to get a plant to grow
you have to be patient. Take your time,
make it slow." She's crouched beside beds
full of sweet potatoes & beans. Cherry
tomatoes, okra, peppers & squash. "Imagine
a future that doesn't even exist yet. Trust
there will be a tomorrow & a day after that."
Her knees splinter & crack. Palms covered
in soil. She passes me veggies, places my hands
in the dirt. "There's not a thing scary
about the unknown. Not a thing to fret
about what's to come. You just work
with all you've got and look for all
the goodness to arrive."

Harvest Party

Mamaw, Mom & I host the biggest dang
harvest party in the whole neighborhood.

Everyone's invited. Doors thrown open,
music on high volume. The Commodores

& Dolly Parton blast the entire block. Hips
shake & hands are thrown to the sky.

This garden can feed the county, come
on, grab a bag & fill it to the brim. "Come

hungry and leave full," she says. Props open
the screen door, fills the cooler with ice.

Mariella's folks bring BBQ chicken. Her
sister joins too, shows us all the moves.

Someone starts the Electric Slide, & all feet
hit the grass dance floor. Mom's mood

is lifted. Summer's officially over; school
will keep me more than occupied forever,

or that's what it feels like. She can see
my whole life, me already on my way.

She hugs me around the neck, whispers
how proud she is, but I haven't even started.

I pack bags overflowing with vegetables. Eggplants
& fennel for days. Hand out Mamaw's recipes.

Neither of them knows how scared I am, terrified
of fitting in. Belonging anywhere besides

this backyard. StaceyAnn & Mariella beside me.
Can't see myself anyplace else. & worried

no one will see me when I show up.

Mom Says

"Even though middle school sometimes
stinks, you'll make it. You'll thrive.
Keep your head all the way up."

Don't:
Worry about what other kids say.
Worry about what you look like.
Stress out about what other kids have.
Get in your head too much.

Do:
Your homework every night. Breathe.
Make sure the teachers know your name.
Spend time with the friends you love.
Focus on yourself & your own brilliant mind.
Listen to what Mamaw & I tell you.

Take it easy. Relax, Beatrice.
We've been there before, & we know
exactly what we're talking about.

Mamaw Promises

We can work it out.
No matter what happens.
Life is very short,
& we've got you every step
of every way.
Don't you worry about one
little thing. Not one.
We'll be the shelter
in your rain. Cover you
& protect you.
Put your trust in me, us.

You know what you are—
the sunshine of my life.
& I mean it from the very
bottom of my heart.

It takes me a few minutes
to realize that Mamaw
is just repeating
her favorite lyrics
from her most beloved
Stevie Wonder songs.

"Ah, Mamaw, come on." I sigh.

"Well, if Stevie said it best,
then why do I need to re-create
what it is I want to say?
Besides, I promise you
nothing will happen in middle school
that can't be fixed by playing a song
by Stevie Wonder. Mark my words.
Now, try and get some sleep.
Tomorrow's a big day.
Don't be so uptight.
Everything is all right."

Garden at Midnight

Night
blooming
jasmine pulls
me in. I rise
middle of the night
wide sky holding above
rest of the house calm, silent
so quiet I tiptoe outside
put my whole face to the flowering,
smell the very deep end of summer.

Try to adjust who I'm supposed to be
roll my shoulders back, face all the stars
count everything I'm thankful for
my mom, my mamaw, my heart
& how it loves so hard
& don't forget luck
wrap my arms around
myself
tight.

Mom = All Buttoned Up
Mamaw = All the Way Let Loose

Before school, Mom wants me neat & presentable.
Hair combed, face washed, teeth brushed, clothes ironed.

Mamaw has never ironed an article of clothing
in her whole life. I'm not even sure she could pick one out
of a lineup of home goods.

She's all loose all the time. Mamaw cares more
about the inside, that's for sure,
& making certain I have homemade bread
laced with rosemary and Himalayan salt,
garden tomatoes with cucumber.
A salad on bread for breakfast.

Says the ways I take care of the insides
will make my outside shine.

"Not if she's full of crumbs and wearing a wrinkled top,"
Mom says, shoving me out the door & into the car.
"And especially not if she's late
for her first day of school."

"Well, run along, you two. But don't worry so much. You know what I always say . . . Time is a . . ."

"CONSTRUCT," we shout.

Mom Slams the Car Door

"Just so you know. Time is real.
It's really 8:02 a.m. right now.
And you are currently late
and I am actually tired
and tired of your mamaw
constantly coming up against the way
I'm trying to raise you.
You really woke up at 7:37
and your mamaw truly insisted
on making you a fresh farm-raised
organic fried egg at 7:42,
which means you
didn't get to wash your face
or brush your teeth at 7:53,
and she definitely got the chance
to tell us that time is a construct.
Well, let me tell you something.
No matter what any of her kooky
or wild healers or mystics tell her
or you or me, I am here to tell you
that time is real. It's real. I'm real.
You're real. And I'm really fed up."

In My Head

Sure, time is not a construct
but does any of that really matter?
What matters is that it's Day #1
of school. & whether time
is real or not, the zit on my chin
is real. I really tried to pop it
this morning & made it worse.
Of course! The story of my life.
& I really am wearing a wrinkled top
& barely had time to get my books
& get my looks together.

At drop-off, Mom pulls me in for a hug
& tells me she's sorry that she keeps
losing her temper. She doesn't even
know why. I hug back & try to catch
my reflection in the rearview.

"Have a great first day of school,
sweet, sweet Beatrice! Love you always."

Alternate Names for the Seventh Grade

The Place Where No One Knows My Name
The Place Where Everyone (Except Me) Knows One Another
Middle of Nowhere
Nowheresville
Foreheads, Butts & Other Awkward Body Parts
Pee on EVERY Toilet Seat
Place of Dirty Bathrooms & Stinky Classrooms
Land of Repugnant Lunches
Body Odor & Sweat Heaven
Does ANYONE Know What Deodorant Is?!
Land of Hormones
Puberty Land
Land of Changing Bodies
Place I Can't Escape
Science & Math & HELPPPPPPP!
Not Elementary School Anymore
Not What Your Mom Said It Would Be
Not What Your Mamaw Promised

New Faces & Names

There are exactly twenty-eight of us in homeroom. Faces
& names that are new to me. We wear name tags
to define who we are. The correct spelling, perfect
pronunciation, say them in my head like a chant.
As if I'm casting some spell. Abdul, Alejandro,
Alexia, Avery, Benjamin, Brianna, Chloe,
Dante, Darnell, Ebony, Eliza, Guadalupe, Henry,
José, Jessica, Katie, Liam, Lucas, Malik, Mariella, Miles,
Nicole, Noah, Olivia, Penelope, Rodney & StaceyAnn.

Not all of us look as scared as I am. But some of us
look even more scared. Wide eyes & heads rested
on palms. Shoulders slumped. To me, looks like
some of us are trying to fit in by not calling too
much attention to ourselves. & some of us
are calling lots of attention to ourselves.
All of us hoping for the same results. To see
& be seen. For who we are & who we want
to be.

Where We're From

When Ms. Berry, our new poetry teacher,
asks us to tell her where we are from, we whine
& say: *Here. Kentucky. Nowhere.* But she pushes on.
Says, "What foods and people and places make you *you*?"

She gives us parameters. Some kind of constraints,
she calls them. Says, "Tell me in ten lines,
three-word sentences. Go on, try."

Beatrice
Bluegrass-born Beatrice.
My name's corny.
Still love Mamaw.
Cornbread & butter.
My whole life.
Ancestors all Irish.
Maybe Scottish, too.
Never been anywhere.
Love orange soda.
Garden veggie feast.

Mariella
Born: Puebla, Mexico.
Mole for life.
Bilingual for life.

Bicultural for life.
Mexican flag flying.
Church is everything.
Missing home always.
Kentucky's still funky.
Don't always belong.
Miss my cousins.
Miss the sunshine.
Love StaceyAnn, Beatrice.

"I know it's more than ten lines,
but I had more to say," Mariella begs,
handing over her poem.

StaceyAnn

Dad = Black.
Mom = white.
Me = mixed.
I know myself.
I define me.
Complicated country girl.
Farmers, factory workers.
I'm from everywhere.
Represent the world.
My own story.

Social Misfits

That's what we call ourselves.
Mariella, StaceyAnn & me.
The three mini musketeers.
Caped crusaders of cool.
Okay, I made that last one up.
But we're a team.
Awkward on the outside,
hip & smooth
on the inside.
We say it when we hang out
& when we make silly videos.
& on the phone
before we hang up.
Social Misfits!
Social Misfits!
Social Misfits Unite!

What Everyone Except Me Knows

Malik knows all the answers.
Mariella knows all the answers.
José knows all the answers in English & Spanish.
Alexia speaks French & Italian at home
& English when she talks to me.
& even with all those different ways
to say the words swirling wild through her head,
she *still* knows all the answers.

I stay asking questions,
the kind no one else ever thinks to ask.
Why do zits have terrible attitudes
& land on my face like they're trying to move in?
How much oil can occupy the bridge of my nose
before I drown? Will I ever look in the mirror
& really, really love what I see? When people look at me,
who do they see? What does grown-up feel like?
Will I always be a kid somehow? What if
everyone grows up without me & I stay stuck?
Will my outside ever match what I feel inside?

The Average Day in Middle School

8 a.m.: arrive early, since Mom does drop-off
as soon as she gets off her shift. Pretend to blend.
Sit near your locker. You still can't remember
the combination. Play clueless, then play smart. *Ugh.*
Eat second breakfast. Waffle sticks & syrup.
Pretend the rest of the day will be this sweet.

8:15 a.m.: homeroom. Keep memorizing. Names
scroll through your head. Say them when you
ask for a pencil, extra eraser. Mistakes keep
happening & you want ways to make them fade.
Dissolve right before your eyes.

8:30 a.m.: Ms. Harrison for English language arts.
Ms. Berry for special poetry class once a week.
Love reading. Love books. Love disappearing.
Love words. Love blank pages. Love fairy tales.
Love fiction. Love poetry. Love storytelling.

9:15 a.m.: five minutes between classes to: pee,
never poop (I would truly rather EVAPORATE
than poop in the middle school bathroom).
People have done it before, but they never
returned.

10 a.m.: science with Mr. Brady. He loves building
community. But clearly likes boys the most. Says
things like: "Lucas, Malik, Avery, Darnell, Henry,
you got it." "Correct." "Right again." "Well done."
"So, so, so, so smart." My hand doesn't always go up,
but even when it does, it feels like it flies right
up & off my arm. Me = melting.

10:45 a.m.: Español. Mi nombre es Beatrice, excepto
que mi nombre en español es Margarita.
Lo elegí para ser cool. No creo que esté funcionando.
Buenos días. Mariella habla con fluidez, así que me siento
a su lado y pretendo no hacer trampa.
Pero definitivamente estoy haciendo trampa.

Google Translation: my name is Beatrice,
except my Spanish name is Margarita.
I picked it to be cool. I do not think it is working.
Good morning. Mariella is fluent so I sit
next to her and pretend not to cheat.
But I am definitely cheating.

11:30 p.m.: LUNCH. Praise God, or the universe, or each
goddess, the way Mamaw does in our garden every
morning. I spend all day waiting for this moment. Order

extra gravy on my mashed potatoes & extra cheese
on my pineapples. Bardstown, Kentucky, lunches are
eccentric & delicious in their own ways.
Mariella & StaceyAnn sit close so we feel like we could
actually survive.

12 p.m.: sink back into social studies. The world. Where
we live & how we live in it. Think: Why did you eat
so much at lunch? Think: How in the actual world
am I supposed to keep my eyes open? Head nodding,
swallowed up by the droning.

12:55 p.m.: nurse's office. Text: I swear, I think I'm sick.
Cold sweats, tired & achy all over. Fever, I'm sure,
flu season is upon us. Stomachache. Sore throat, sniffles.
Subtext: "Don't make me go to gym. Rather perish. Pass
all the way away. Gym + me = death every time. Death
by soccer ball. Death by volleyball. Death by anything
that includes a ball. Please send me home early?!"

Nurse's response: *You're fine.*

1 p.m.: gym—NOOOOOOOO!!!!!

2 p.m.: math + Beatrice = same as gym but worse. Sit
as far back as possible. Deep breaths. Cease to exist.

2:45 p.m.: bell rings. Still can't remember
locker combination. Names still muddled.

Find Mariella.

Find StaceyAnn.

Find ways to exist again.

Bardstown Baked

Takes up a whole block on Third Street downtown,
next to Benny's Barber Shoppe & Hurst Drugstore.
Mamaw's been working here going on twenty years.
She calls it: a staple. We call it: delicious.
Mariella & StaceyAnn & I pretend to study here,
& every day, Mamaw slips us molasses & oatmeal
cookies, chocolate chunk & walnut surprise.
Sometimes she'll make us her Bluegrass Elixir
with coffee, extra milk & caramel swirl, or better,
a slice from one of her fancy cakes like bourbon
funfetti or Kentucky crumble loaded with raspberries.
Mamaw calls it "old hand," but we call it "experimental."
A sea of tarts & muffins & almond croissants that melt
upon first taste. We call it "heaven" sometimes.
The ultimate reset after a day in middle school hell.

The Boys in My Class

Sometimes the boys in my class
think their voices are smarter & louder & more polished.
They think they shine—brighter, bolder. Sometimes
one of their voices starts, and the others join up.
So they sound just like a chorus.

Lucas talks louder than all of them.
It's like his voice is a trophy
& he spends all his time polishing it
& finding the perfect spot to display it.
Loudly!
& Mr. Brady seems to like his the most,
because he's always calling on him.
Lucas, what do you think? Lucas,
how do you feel about it? Let's start with you,
Lucas.

Sometimes, the louder his voice gets,
the quieter mine becomes.

Body Moves

My body moves sometimes—without me.
In my mind, I'll be thinking,
Walkcoolbecoolactcoollookcoolpretendcoolplaycool
coolcoolcoolcoolcoolcoolcoolcoolcoolcoolcoolcoolcool.
And then just like that—as soon as I'm all
ice cube, pool in the summer, Popsicle, snow globe,
freezing rain, twenty degrees, freezer full of ice cream,

just like that—my body goes lopsided & loose,
goes all Gumby & stretches when it's supposed to glide
& fidgets when it's supposed to be calm & stumbles
when it's supposed to be smooth. & worst of all
is that it does all this clumsy & uncontrollable
in front of the people I want to be so coolcoolcool
in front of.

Lunchroom Catastrophe

Just like that, I fall. In the lunchroom. In front of

EVERYONE!

Nightmares do in fact come true.
Here I am, piling my tray.
Salisbury steak & mashed potatoes,
double rolls (because they're heavenly),
corn loaded with butter & salt,
& a very large piece of chocolate cake.

Most of the time, our lunch is super healthy,
but some of the time, the folks who cook
get a little wild & let loose their skills.
They forget about calorie counting
& good for your heart. Mamaw says
the cooks in the lunchroom are Southern
to the bone & still cooking with salt + fat + love.
She knows most of them, which is why
my slice of cake is currently overflowing.
I am planning to share with my crew
when I exit the line too fast
& my milk carton tips over,
tilting too close to my feast.

I lean to the left, then twist right
& get caught up in my complete lack
of coordination, twisting one foot behind
the other & buckling under the weight
of keeping everything balanced.

CRASH
CLASH
CLATTER
CLANG
SMASH
THUNDER

A P P L A U S E!

It's such a cliché, but people do in fact
start to clap. A tradition
when anyone drops or spills anything
in any way. StaceyAnn sees me first
& runs over to help me up. So does Abdul,
who is standing right behind me.
I gather my tray & pile what's left
of my food & my pride together.
StaceyAnn whispers in my ear, "Take a bow."
I look at her like she's wilder than I thought.
"Trust me. Take. A. Deep. Bow," she urges, nudging me.

I stop the tears from bursting out of my eyes,
take a small step forward & gesture the biggest
& goofiest flourish I can think of, bending down
all the way. A breathtaking bow for my adoring
fans. The crowd actually & in real time goes wild.
People yahoo & roar. A symphony because of me,
for me, about me. Either way, I am both wilting
& coming alive inside.

Alternate Names for the Bathroom

The place where I go
to cry
hide
stare
disappear behind a closed door.

The place that never
has enough
soap
toilet paper
sanitizer
sanity
doors that actually close
locks that actually lock.

The place
where
no one
looks for me.

The place
I don't want
anyone
to find me.

Are You Okay?

Is the thing Rodney says
when I walk out of the bathroom.

"Are you talking to me?" I ask,
looking behind me.
He can't be talking to me. Can he?

"Yeah, I, uh . . . just wanted to make sure
you weren't hurt or anything.
You fell pretty hard back there."

Yes, he is talking to me. Did he follow me?
No, he couldn't have followed me.

"I followed you to make sure everything was okay.
You were in the bathroom for a while
so I just . . . I wanted to make sure."

He was following me. OMG.

"Oh, you mean that little fall back there?
Oh, that was nothing. I fall all the time."
What are you even saying?!

"Oh, good. I just figured someone
should come and check on you.
I mean, it sucks," he says,
throwing his arms out.
"If only we had those superpowers,
you know? Fast healing, invisibility,
either of those would've worked."

"Yeah, I could've really used invisibility
back there." *I could really use invisibility
ALL THE TIME.*

He pushes his dark, wavy hair away from his face
& smiles so wide it makes his eyes
light up. & his smile makes me smile too.

Well, maybe not all the time.

Supernatural Powers & Abilities

After school, I sit with Rodney outside
while he waits for his dad to pick him up.
He pulls out a wrinkled piece of paper
& shares it with me.
"Here's my list," Rodney says.

Types of Powers: Top Ten
1. Aquatic Breathing—easily my favorite.
2. Poison Immunity—who wants to be poisoned?!
3. Hyperawareness—I need to know where
   I am & who I am at all times.
4. Enhanced Senses—again, always aware.
   Also super taste for fried chicken—check.
5. Night Vision—who doesn't want to see
   in the dark?
6. Botanical Communication—I like plants.
7. Clairvoyance—seeing the future would be rad.
8. Flight—obvious.
9. Enhanced Lung Capacity—would help with
   gym.
10. Hybrid Soul—I just really like the sound
    of that one.

"You can keep it. I have another copy.
Besides, they kind of keep changing

depending on my mood."

He hands it over & I study it close.

"What do you think would be on your list?"

Turns Out

Falling in the lunchroom is actually kind of a cool move.
A way to get everyone talking about you, at least.
Chloe, Eliza, Brianna & Olivia say hi & invite me to sit
at their table. The circular one in the middle.
Not the ones on the sidelines—
the ones that get pushed away.
They are the center. That's where they sit.
In science class, they would be: the nucleus. It's true.
They are the sun & we're all just revolving around them.

I say yes the day when Mariella & StaceyAnn are out.
Both of them at a meeting for the soccer team. Not me.
I play zero sports during the school year. I sit. Stay silent.
Try & make conversation, but it goes something like this.

"That fall was ahhh-mazing," Olivia says.
(*Not really,* I think but say nothing, just nod.)

"How in the world did you do that?"
(Uhhh, it was super easy, I just
tripped over my own two feet.)

"I loved that you just bowed—like you didn't even care."
(I TOTALLY cared. Still care. Caring currently.
And the bow was totally StaceyAnn's idea.

Can't take credit for that one.
Also—it's what they do in all the old movies
my mom makes me watch, so there's that.)

"What do you do on the weekends?"
(Hmm . . . garden with my mamaw
& play games with my best friends.)

"You should sit with us more often," Eliza says.
"Yeah," I finally say, finding my voice.
"That'd be cool."

I spend the rest of the lunch nodding & smiling along.
They seem to kind of like me but have no idea
who I really am.
I guess that's partly
because I'm trying to figure that out myself.

Hands Down

Lunch is still my favorite part of the day, & when it's chili
& chicken noodle soup, I'm glowing. A type of food heaven
Mamaw says exists only if you love life enough to eat it alive.

I do. They serve pimento cheese or peanut butter with honey.
Mamaw says this is what the South is all about.
Recipes for building muscles & heart. She tells me to eat
with your whole body. Learn to love the time it takes
to make something from scratch. Homemade.
Says food is joy, is communion, is what it takes
to always bring you back to the table.

On these days, she slips me two dollars for extra honey.
She knows I need all the sweet I can get.

All Morning Long

I stay steady daydreaming. Blame
the window to the left of me & the fact
it faces sky & lawn & so many endless
possibilities outside this dead-end classroom.
Blame Mamaw, who planted all the many wild
ways to be in the world. For sure blame Mariella
& StaceyAnn, who say daydreaming's the best part
of school anyway, so why not spend forever doing it?
Blame Mr. Brady, who speaks sometimes
like a robot & drones & drones & drones on.
Predictions, specific scientific evidence. Blame
Rodney & the way his chin sits in his open palm,
his own daydreams floating up—on top of his head
dancing with mine. But most of all. Blame me
& my own mind. The way it wanders most times
without me. Sees me from space—up above.
& directs me right on up, up, up & into the clouds.

My Dreams Get Lost

I'm a kid again. Playing family & house.
Mariella, StaceyAnn & me building our lives,
the ones we dream about.

"I'll be a doctor who also acts on the side
and a writer who owns a bookstore. I'll own
the bakery where Mamaw works and a house
that fits my whole family. Mom can have her own
room and Mamaw can plant an even bigger garden
and we'll all live together happy and comfortable.
I'll fall in love, of course. Have lots of kids—maybe four
or five—a whole big, sprawling family. Definitely not
one. One kid is too hard. I'm an only child. It's rough
out here alone. On my own. I'll have it all."

Those were the kinds of dreams we had then. But now.
I just want to make it through middle school. Not trip
again. Not bleed through my underwear, not have zits
that cover my chin or my forehead. Get a first kiss maybe
or someone to like me. No one ever likes me. Will anyone
ever like me? I dream that I fit in everywhere.
Everywhere I go. I belong.

Seventh-Grade Dream

I go on & see myself
the way I want to be seen.

"Envision! Envision! Envision!
Anything you make
with your own two hands
is worth it. Anything you make
with your own two hands
is worth it."
Mamaw's mantras float in my head.

This is the year that the boys notice me,
all of me. The year I make *them* daydream
about me. The year they talk about
how funny I am, how laid-back & chill I am,
how they wish I was their girlfriend.
& say things like: *She's the total package*,
whatever that really means. This is the year
that Chloe & Eliza & Olivia & Brianna
decide they need a fifth member of the crew
& invite me in. The year they finally see
that a slumber party is not the same without me
& that I'm the perfect addition to their squad.
The year I finally become part of a "squad"
rather than a social misfit, even though I love

Mariella & StaceyAnn. It's time to be seen.
Time to shine.

This is the year I'm named most popular,
most talented, class president, most stylish,
best laugh, prettiest smile, best body
(okay, I know, I know that's not an actual
yearbook category, but still).
I would like to have the best body, the best legs,
the best hair, the best everything, anything.
I'll take it! All of it.

It's Day of the Girl

My teacher Ms. Harrison says. & she's always,
always talking in exclamation points. She says things
like: "Seriously, you should know this! & Have you ever
stopped to think? & What do you think of this? & You
will never believe it & I'm telling you right now!
& Believe me when I say! & Truth be told! & Do you know
what I am trying to say? & Mark my words!"

& seriously, she should know that she makes my brain
feel like it's in a hard-core gymnastics class. Gymnastics,
another sport I'm crap at. But back to my brain. My
elastic, bombastic, energetic, ecstatic, electric brain.

The one that's been my best company for twelve years.
But lately it feels jumbled when I try & say
what's inside it.
Sometimes there's too much up there,
& I stumble around letting my insecurities
bubble up to the top, without me.

You All Have Beautiful Voices

So you should use them as much as possible!"
Ms. Harrison says. "Your voices are bridges
that connect you to the world. Your voices
are oceans collecting all your visions
& ideas & washing them to the shore.
Your voices are anchors & pulleys,
ships & buoys. Always, your voices
are the tallest trees in the forest.
They rise up. They are canopies & shelter.
Balm & salve. They can heal & calm.
Use them to build yourselves up & help others
climb toward who they're meant to be.
Your voices are magic! The kind
that mends & cures, rejuvenates
& renews. *Go on and use them, use them
up until all I hear is a chorus of breath!"*

First of All

I have no idea what Ms. Harrison is talking about
most of the time. She is at least a billion years old
or that's what she told us last week, laughing.
& THEN, she had us make metaphors & similes
with the idea of old. You know:

As old as the hills (that's a massive cliché, by the way)
Old as when dinosaurs ruled the land
Old like shoes that have run a hundred miles
Old as the sea
As old as history.

& then! She had us use her as an example—

Ms. Harrison is a fossil (she really howled at this one)
Ms. Harrison is a cool antique you find at a flea market
Ms. Harrison is a dusty old-fashioned book you find in
your attic.

"Full of knowledge, I'm sure," Ms. Harrison said.
"I'm seventy-two & counting.
That's nearly sixty years older than you.
& you might be wise to listen to what I have to say."

So I've pretty much decided she's a wild genius
& even though I'm almost always lost in her class,
I figure she knows the best ways out.

Alternate Names for Gym Class

The Stinky Pit
Laugh Factory
House of My Sadness
Volleyball Drama
The Place Where No One Scores
The Home Run to Nowhere
Slam Dunk Me in the Face
Goal: Never Again
Destination: Spikesville
The Place Where I Dribble the Ball Alone
House of My Sorrows
(that one seems a little dramatic, but still)
Jump Rope Disaster
(which is my current favorite,
since I tripped during the fitness test last week
& busted my lip in front of the whole class & God,
who I don't even know if I believe in,
especially since I can't think of any good God
that would invent gym class
& then make me completely miserable at it).

My List of Superpowers

1. Chaos Manipulation—so I can confuse
   the gym teachers & they can never find me.
2. Enigma Force—so everyone will want to be
   close to me, near me.
3. Emotion Vision—to figure out how everyone
   around me is feeling so I don't have to guess.
4. Supernatural Strength—always first place.
5. Healing Vision—my favorite.
6. Telepathy—so I can read minds, especially
   Rodney's mind. What is he thinking?
   What is he feeling? I must know.
7. Rainbow Manipulation—I'm not exactly sure
   what that entails, but I want it. Badly.
8. Age Manipulation—MUST GROW UP.
9. Teleportation—could I get to high school
   already?
10. Self-Detonation—in case I ever make a fool out
    of myself . . . again.

I make a whole list to match Rodney's
& I almost give it to him.
But at the last second,
I chicken out.
Maybe being brave
should be at the very top
of the list of superpowers I really wish I had.

Egomania

"That's what we're learning today," Mr. Brady says,
all egotistical, as if he's mastered the art already.
"Brag," he says, drawing out the word.
"Show us who you are!"

Some of the boys shout out, their voices flying
from their mouths.

Freshest, astonishing,
otherworldly, godly,
spectacular, miraculous,
fantastic, brilliant,
towering, awesome,
stupendous, superb.
As if they've been waiting their whole lives
to tell about how magnificent they are.

Mr. Brady looks at us. Silent. Mariella is quiet, reading
her YA novel tucked tight into her desk. She thinks
she's slick. & StaceyAnn is curling the letters in her name.

I'm busy drawing a highly realistic rendition of myself
vomiting in a trash can, my hair a puff of cotton candy
around my angelic face. & the vomit really spewing
& spinning from my mouth. Sure, it's immature.

But it's a JOKE! If Mr. Brady doesn't understand that,
then he has no sense of humor whatsoever.

Turns out, Mr. Brady has no sense of humor whatsoever.
& neither does our principal, Ms. Shipman.
Or the counselor, Ms. Rodriguez.
Except I think she kind of understands when I say,

"Sometimes I feel like the people who talk the most
do the least amount of work."

Trouble

"You simply cannot draw yourself vomiting in class,"
Mamaw starts. Mom is nodding in the background.
"And then get caught. You have to be more careful."

"Or how about not do it at all?" Mom jumps in.

"Oh, right. That's true," Mamaw adds, then mouths
don't get caught at me again for emphasis.

They're both irritated. Annoyed when they got the call
from the counselor to ask if everything
was okay at home, & furious when I lied
& said I didn't do anything wrong.

I didn't think Mr. Brady would do a follow-up phone call
to try & pretend he cares about my well-being.
He does not.

"You've had a strong start to the year, Beatrice.
Let's keep it that way," Mom adds.

"I'm sorry," I say. "I know I shouldn't have done it.
I was just tired of everyone else having the answer,
especially the boys. And feeling like I never, ever
know the right things to say."

Mamaw & Mom stare at me now, which seems like neither of them knows the right things to say, either.

In Other News

We stay silent until Mom says she has something to say,
a question she's been meaning to ask us.

Mamaw & I look up, surprised. "What's on your mind?"
Mamaw asks.

"Well, I know this is not the perfect time to bring this up,
but I figure now or never. And since Beatrice is grounded
and will be staying with us all weekend . . ."

Now I'm getting nervous. What is she trying to say?

"I met someone," Mom starts.

Harrison Douglas immediately flashes in my mind.
Why in the world didn't I return to my Google search?!
Who is he? And how did he get a place in Mom's heart?

"His name is Harrison Douglas. I met him at the hospital.
He's in medical sales, and he is kind, funny, and single."
Mom starts to laugh a little at this, which is strange.
Is she embarrassed? Nervous? She must really like him.

Mamaw's eyebrows have absolutely not left
the tip-top of her forehead. They're stuck up there.

She's smiling, but I can tell this is new.
Besides the occasional date, Mom has been single,
just the three of us. & since Mom's folks passed away
a few years back, it truly is just Mamaw, Mom & me.
This is new territory for everyone.

"What I'm saying is . . . I would like you both to meet him.
I never ask this unless it's serious, but this feels like
it could be. Would you both come to dinner?"

I'll Cook

This is what Mamaw says immediately.
"Let's make him a homemade meal.
Beatrice will help. Show him who we are."

"I love that idea, but he really wants to treat.
He wants to take us all to Bourbon House."
Mom says this with emphasis, knowing
it's the fanciest restaurant in town.
We've never been.

"Bourbon House!" Mamaw exclaims.
"My goodness. Is he rich?!" She laughs.
"That's much too expensive. No thank you."

"Bea, please?" Mom looks at me for help.
"I would love for you and Beatrice to meet him,
give him a chance. I don't ask much of you,
but I am asking this."

"Come on, Mamaw. It will be fun," I say,
kicking myself for not knowing more
about this two-last-named man.
Trying to keep an open mind
but panicking on the inside.

"Fine, fine. I'll go for you two. But I will not
like it. Not one bit. When is this happening?"

"Tomorrow night," Mom says.

"I'll get dressed up," Mamaw replies.

Mom gives me a worried look,
because Mamaw dressed up
could truly mean anything.

Mamaw's Outfit

Is outrageous! In a funny & altogether over-the-top
kind of way. I'm pretty sure it's on purpose
as she floats down the stairs in her tie-dyed skirt
& faux-leopard-print fur jacket, feathered earrings
dangling from both ears. She has layers upon layers
& her hair is a nest framing her face, combed out
so it's a puff of fluff. She poses & pauses on the steps.
Mom almost loses her breath when she sees her.
I give Mom a look that says: *You asked for this.*
Let Mamaw be Mamaw or we're gonna have problems.

I've seen Mamaw throw tantrums when asked
to act a certain way. I've seen her lay it on thick
when she thinks people underestimate who she is.
It's a delicate balance with her, & we do not
want to disrupt her essence.

"You both look great," is what Mom says.

I look down at my outfit, which is tame
compared to Mamaw's. A dress from Goodwill
with leggings and boots underneath.
Mamaw puts her arm around me.

"We certainly do," she says,
just as the doorbell rings.

Reasons Harrison Douglas Is Suspect

His hair is not cool, as Mom first described.
It's ludicrous. Puffs up & out on his head,
shaped in what Mamaw calls a bouffant.
He gels it all just right. You can tell.
He definitely spends a whole lot of time
in front of the mirror perfectly perfecting
his slicked-back 'do.
He's also got a snobby attitude.
I can tell right away.
See him raise his eyebrows
at our secondhand sofa & how it's covered
in all of Mamaw's multicolored quilts.
& yes, I know just as well as anyone
that Mamaw's *very* abstract paintings of her garden
& my elementary school drawings
hanging up in frames around the house
look clunky & mismatched
& that nothing at all in our house
looks done up or polished.
We are all rough around the edges,
but it's our house,
& yes, it's small,
but the better to hear each other
& love each other.
& yeah, it's funky & eclectic & unique

just like all of us, but the funky is ours
& ours alone.
& I know for certain
that there is not one ounce
of room
for Harrison
or any of his many hair products.

Mamaw Says

"Give him a chance," as we walk to the car.

She's all, "Hi, Harrison. How are you?
We've heard sooo much about you.
Can't wait to hear about your job and you.
And how you and Lisa met. Tell us everything."

What in the world is Mamaw doing?!

"Let's do this for your mother," Mamaw insists,
making me think that Mom
might really need this
& us
to be on our very best behavior.

At Dinner

Mamaw guffaws at the menu,
points at the overpriced everything
& says, "I'll just have a salad."

Mom gives both of us another one of her looks.

"Fine, I'll have the vegetable plate with brussels sprouts,
mashed potatoes, and garlic green beans,"
Mamaw orders.

"You should order the steak—rare,"
Harrison says.

"I'm a vegetarian," Mamaw answers.
"Truth is, meat is destroying the planet,
especially beef," she finishes,
even though sometimes she slips,
& has a pepperoni or two
or a few bites of bacon.
I can tell, she's not sharing that information
with Harrison Douglas.

So much for giving him a chance.

"I'll just have the burger," I say,
trying to fold my napkin on my lap just right.

"Yes, please, order anything. I love this place.
It's really the only nice place in town
if you want my opinion."

I *do not* want his opinion.

"Lisa tells me you all have never been here.
I'm so happy to treat. Lisa has told me so much
about both of you. I can't wait to find out more."

& then he starts talking. Actually, he starts
monologuing. You know, when someone yacks
on & on without stopping. It's funny.
He said he wants to know more about us,
but all he's talking about is HIM!
We find out . . .

where he grew up, who his family is
what he loves to do in his spare time
how fast he can run a mile
his favorite sports in middle school
his favorite sports in high school
his favorite sports currently
his favorite places to *dine*
how good he is with money
all the places he has traveled
all the places he wants to travel

when he plans to retire
where he hopes to live.

By the end of his speech, Mamaw is rolling
her eyes directly at me. Looks like we gave him
a good enough chance.

Cincinnati

"It's really the best city. I can't say enough about it.
I mean, it's an actual city, not like Louisville or
Lexington. Those are just big towns
that are trying to pretend.
I've been telling your mom it would be a perfect place
to raise you."

At this, Mamaw's face goes cold.

"Oh, Beatrice is being raised just fine
right here in Bardstown. We've got family and friends
and a big garden." She makes a gesture
in the direction of our house. I can tell
she is ready to get out of here.

Harrison Douglas smirks, or at least
that's what it looks like to me.
A slow curl inches its way up.

"Don't get me wrong:
Bardstown is a great small town,
but there's just no real culture here.
In Cincinnati, you can go see a show,
visit a museum, eat foods from around the world.

Raising kids in cities makes them more . . . I don't know,
worldly . . . sophisticated. I mean, look at me."
He grins again & reaches for Mom's hand.

She smiles over at me, somehow under his spell.

"You never know," Mom says.

I Sure as Hell Know

I don't like him."
That's what Mamaw says.

Side note: Mamaw curses.
Not all the time & not too much,
but to her, curse words
offer an extra flair.
She says they're just words.
& that real curse words
are the ones that hurt people
& a little "hell" or "damn"
here & there
can help make a point.
I get it.
& agree.

"Acting like we can't raise you."

"That's not what he said," I say.

"It's what he implied, though,
isn't it? Cincinnati. Please!
I know a fake when I see one,
& Harrison Douglas
just happens to be
one of them."

The Fight

"I heard that," Mom calls from the kitchen,
making her way to us. "That's enough."
She is talking to Mamaw now. "I like him,
Beatrice likes him"—I don't disagree at this moment—
"and I think I know what's best for this family.
Not you." Mom puts her emphasis there
& I get a sick feeling in my stomach.
She's wrong about that. It's the three of us
working together, living & building together.

"He's not good enough for you," Mamaw says,
standing up now, her loud skirt piled around her.
"And he's not good enough for us either."

"Bea, I am tired of you telling me what to do
and how you think I should raise Beatrice
and always commenting on what I'm messing up
and what I'm doing wrong. Nothing is ever
good enough for you. And you think no one
is ever good enough for me,"
Mom says, her eyes filling with tears.
"At least not since . . ." We all know what comes next.
The death. The one that floats over all of us,
the one that creeps into my dreams
& hangs over my waking hours,

the one Mamaw keeps carried in photographs
that cover the walls in our home. Her son.
Mom's husband. My dad. Like a ghost.

"Well, excuse me for wanting the best
for all of us. You are absolutely correct.
Have it your way. I will stay out of it."

She up & walks away, leaving us both
lost & confused.

Give Him a Chance

Mom is curled up in bed with me.
She smells like her favorite perfume
& jasmine fills my whole bedroom.

"I know this is new," she says,
"but you and your mamaw will come around.
I know it." I try to burrow down even deeper.

When I was a baby, Mom tells it
I would say, "I want to go home,"
when I was sad or upset,
referring to her belly
where I lived for nine months
cuddled & safe in her womb.

"Everything feels new and different,"
I say, looking up at her. My mom
could not be more beautiful.
I think of her sacrifices
& how she has struggled
to make a home for Mamaw & me.
How we've become her all.

"He makes me happy," Mom says.

"I know."

"Don't you want me to be happy?"

Dreaming

Asleep, I dream of a wedding, but instead
of celebration & tears of joy, I'm there
in the corner, alone. Weeping & begging
Mom to stay.

Harrison Douglas is there, but he's not a man.
He's a robot with a tail, & he's standing on a podium
talking & talking & talking until his tongue falls out.

This is no dream. It's a nightmare. & Mamaw is there,
cawing like a bird & shouting to stop the wedding.
There are no roses, just trees that cover us all.

I wake up in a cold sweat, panic settling on in.

The next morning, Mom announces a trip,
says she's going away with Harrison Douglas
in a couple of weeks. Says he loved meeting us.
Says he can see them together. & so can she.

My nightmare come true. Ahhhhhh!

Says, "Wish me luck."

Tree House Reality

The next morning, I ride my bike slow & steady.
All alone, I have time to think about my dreams
& the nightmare that woke me up. Scared & restless.
I tell Mom & Mamaw I have some reading to do
& head to our secret, sacred space. With no one around,
the quiet becomes like company. Open my backpack,
take out two thick slices of Mamaw's homemade bread
slathered in salted butter with apricot jam. Settle in
& let the cool air wash right over me. Take out my list
of superpowers, study it close. Find a groove just behind
the tree. I fold it up & tuck it inside so no one can see
just how badly I want what I don't have. Shut my eyes,
try to truly see the dream me. There she is. So close,
she's almost real.

Top-10 Girls

That's what I call them when the list makes its way
around & I see their names. There are four total.
Chloe. Eliza. Brianna & Olivia. All with top-10 scores.

The sheet of paper says: *Body, Face & Whole Package.*
Bold letters & words written by losers. I'm in a mood
& already fed up with everything. What started
with Harrison Douglas is ending
with Lucas Jones.
& suddenly that dream me
comes crashing down
all around.

He starts the list going around in chorus class.
It feels like a hurricane or tsunami. Paper flailing
through the aisles. How hot can hot be? Fire & heat.

The list circulates to me, & then I see it. My name.

Beatrice Miller. Body = 3 | Face = 1 | Whole Package =

Nothing. At least that's how I feel when I see it. Wasted
drowning from shame. Embarrassment like a close friend
I keep inviting to the boring party of my life. There it is
in red ink. The boys have scored all of me. & the tally
is forgettable, unmentionable. Equal to zero. Less than.

Mariella Says

at least you were on the score sheet,
& we laugh at that,
knowing it's not a full-on joke.
It's true. Not every girl
made the list. & the fact I did
makes me closer to cool
than them. In fact,
the Top-10 Girls said, "HI!"
at my locker.
I was too busy
forgetting my combination
& thinking about Mom
& HD (since I can't stand saying his whole name)
& Mamaw
& the way my life seems to be imploding
in on itself,
but I took notice
that they
were taking notice
of me.
But lately
I don't know what cool means.
Or what it looks like.
Who owns cool?
Who made it
so?

StaceyAnn Says

Screw that stupid list. Seriously.
I don't even like boys anyway.
Only my brother & my dad.
Oh & Dante & Rodney are cool too.
Sure, my cousins—Zahir & Richie.
Coach Crenshaw & Coach Blandon,
of course. Coach Malone for soccer.
Oh yeah, my uncle Avery
& uncle Jared & uncle Steve
& my papaw, of course. He's number one—
tells the best stories, makes the best
chili, knows how to win at poker.

But what I mean is, I don't like boys
like that. Like, I don't want to kiss
Lucas or Malik or Noah
or any of the rest of them.
Ever.

You know what I mean.
I don't like boys like that.

Cool, We Say

Listening to StaceyAnn & nodding along
as we try to keep up with her speed. She
races ahead of us only to stop at the corner,
leans back on her bicycle & gives us a look.

Asks, "Are you sure you understand
what I'm trying to tell you? I like girls,"
she says again for emphasis. We nod.
"Ebony, to be specific, but not sure I've got a chance."

"We got it. Cool," I say again, knowing neither
of us cares a lick. Just want StaceyAnn to know
she's our social misfit no matter what.

"I have a crush on Malik," Mariella says.
"And he doesn't even know my name.
Or that I even exist. We're in this together."

I don't tell them I've been day & night dreaming
about Rodney Murphy & the way his hair
swoops across his forehead. I even like
his braces & green rubber bands. His comic-
book T-shirts & his eyebrows that lift up
in a question every time he looks at the board.

Figure I've had enough scoring today
& don't want to find out I'm last place
in the crush department too.

One More Thing

"My mom met someone," I say.
"Awesome," StaceyAnn says.
"That's sooo cool," Mariella adds.
"Is he nice? Is he cute?
What's his name?"

"We hate him," I say.
They both look shocked.
"Okay, okay, we don't *hate* him,
but we really, really, really
don't like him. Like, at all.
And to top it off, she's going
away with him."

"She's moving?" Mariella asks.

"No, no, like for the weekend.
And leaving us on our own."

"I think you gotta stay open-minded.
Let her go. Besides, no one's ever
good enough for the people you love,"
StaceyAnn says, her logic
taking center stage.
She's right. I know she is.

"You should be happy for her."
"I know, I know."

Then why do I still feel like
the biggest loser on the planet
for being sad
about my mom's happiness?

Reasons a Rating System Sucks

Mostly because if someone
gets a 10, then someone
else is definitely
gonna
get
a
1

Rodney Is More than Okay

& here are the reasons why.
He gets super psyched to talk superheroes,
& it's true I love a good save-the-world story.
High flying, death defying, gravity rising.
& it's not just the dudes he's into, although
Miles Morales is his ultimate. & of course
your usuals. Spider-Man, Batman & Green Lantern,
the Flash. But most of all, we deep dive for Katana
& Poison Ivy. Unexpected dialogue, deciding
what Wonder Woman will do next. Starfire
& Bumblebee. Why there aren't more movies
with the leads we want to see. He asks me,
"Have you ever been to the Great Escape? Comic
book nirvana?" And although the answer's no,
I feel like sitting beside Rodney & finding out
his favorite origin story is a kind of dreamland
not unlike a store covered wall-to-wall
with caped crusaders at the ready for rescue.

After School

Mariella, StaceyAnn & I cruise downtown.
Cut across backyards, skip through town,
head straight to Hurst for piling ice-cream cones.
It's October but still warm enough for sweetness,
so we order up our usual. Butter pecan for Mariella.
Strawberry shortcake for StaceyAnn & double
chocolate chunk for me. Two scoops. I'm not scared
of brain freeze or getting full too fast. This is late-fall
tradition. "Let's go to the park to swing," Mariella says,
leading the way. Sometimes I feel all grown-up,
& sometimes I feel like I could be a kid forever.
That's how I feel today as we run ahead, slurping
& shouting. Free & wild.

Then We See Them & Everything Changes

We get almost to the corner when they show up.
Lucas, Liam & Rodney. Crew of boys I wish didn't exist.
Except Rodney, who smiles with his whole mouth
& laughs at most of my jokes.
I don't know what happens,
but when I see them, I freeze, my whole body
an ice cube, but not the cool kind. Evaporating.

"Hey," StaceyAnn calls out.
"Nooo," I say, shove her arm & throw my favorite flavor
in the alley behind us.
"What are you doing?" Mariella asks,
her face a question mark.
When the boys arrive,
I'm the only one empty-handed.
"Hey," Lucas says.
"Hey," Liam says.
"Cool," Rodney says, pointing to their cones.
"None for you?" he says, tilts his head.
I scrunch my face. "Nah. I don't really like ice cream."
I lie . . .
something I've started to get good at doing.
Shame finds its way down the back of my neck
& to my cheeks.
"Too bad," Rodney says. "I love it."

"Bye," Lucas says.

"Bye," Liam says.

"Bye," I call

but realize no sound comes out at all.

Melting

That's how I feel when they walk away. "What was that?"
Mariella & StaceyAnn look at me, their eyes wide open.
"Chocolate chunk is your favorite," they say.
"Two whole scoops gone," they say.
I look behind me, my cone dripping into concrete.
Sweetness seeping silently away. I slump. Slouch.
Can't think of a good enough excuse. Can't say: "Rodney
makes me warm all over." Sweating in fall.
& me wanting to be cool makes me break out in hives.
Cool girls don't eat ice cream & play at the stupid park.
They lean & hang. Like laundry. Fresh & clean.
They're smooth. They don't act like babies.
They know all the right things to say & do.
& chocolate chunk ice cream is most definitely
not on the list.
"It slipped," I say, and even though I know
they don't believe me,
they don't ask me any more questions.

Sometimes I Pretend I'm Dying

Deathbed Beatrice, last leg of hope,
descending this world cloaked & solemn
in a hospital bed. & the whole seventh grade
takes a big yellow school bus
zooming all the way down I-65
to see me—their eyes swollen with tears.
Weeping & wailing.
My condition is so bad,
they keep me quarantined from others
in a fancy room on the top floor.
I don't call it a penthouse . . .
but that's what it is.
& all the doctors scurry around with worry,
racking their brains to discover what ails me.
& the sickness has made my skin totally clear up
& made my hair shine-tastic
so that even though I'm headed to the grave,
I look AMAZING.
& Lucas cries harder than anyone.
So sorry he crushed my feelings.
So do the Top-10 Girls.
Distraught, they tell me how much they've always
loved me.
So does Rodney, who professes his undying crush
on ME—in front of everyone.

& the teachers!
They give speeches about my leadership skills,
my brilliant mind & mostly my heart,
& if I wasn't so weak,
I'd hold them all,
but alas . . . I'm dying.

And then—as if a miracle.
I somehow—against all the odds,
& in direct contrast to my desperate diagnosis,
survive.

Beatrice as Everything She's Not
& Everything She Wants to Be

Today our poetry teacher, Ms. Berry,
does self-portrait poems.
She is all the time telling us:
"You young people love the look of yourselves.
You love to ooohhh and aaahhhh
for the camera's spotlight.
So now it's time to turn those selfies
into perfectly prized poems. Word?"

She's all the time talking in the nineties—
the generation when she grew up.
"Aka the greatest generation," Ms. Berry says.
"Reverse the camera. Show me who you are.
Selfie poem yourselves."
It's easy for her, with her glowing brown skin,
perfectly arched eyebrows & short twists.
She's always saying it's her vegan lifestyle
& exercise that keeps her outside shining.
She sounds just exactly like Mamaw.
So I give it my best shot.

Beatrice swimming freestyle, so fast you can't see her
Beatrice with her hands piled into dirt in her backyard.
Beatrice rocking back & forth on her porch swing,

her mamaw's fingers running through her hair.
Beatrice curled close to her mother in bed,
no nightmares, just dreams, just breathing.
Beatrice on her cool orange cruiser.
Not athletic enough for a ten-speed,
not cool enough for a BMX trick bike.
Beatrice in lotus pose with her mamaw,
who is yoga-ing it out.
Beatrice sometimes crying so hard, she can't even
catch her breath & heaving & heaving
& the Oh My God of it all. Thinking of her mom
& the life she might lead without her mamaw.
Wishing everything could all stay the same,
no change, nothing new. Just stand perfectly still.
Beatrice smiling so hard, her teeth hurt
& eating loads of cheese puffs & downing coffee
with milk & extra sugar.
Beatrice swimming laps at the city pool,
chlorine haze with StaceyAnn & Mariella.
Beatrice laughing until Sprite spills from her nose.
Beatrice hiding under her sheets.
A ghost.
Beatrice sometimes wishing
she could disappear
into thin air.

Beatrice as Superstar

All day I'm trying to be vibrant
& grounded. Planted & growing.
Trying to manage Mom & Mamaw,
my old friends & my new friends
all at the same time. & I feel like
I'm tripping, stumbling into things,
can't get my footing just right.
Chest feeling like a firecracker.
Trying to pretend one moment
& trying to be real the next.
Sometimes it feels like I'm playing
the part of good daughter
& thoughtful granddaughter
& solid friend
but lately my performance
feels like it's unraveling.

Ode to Afternoons Alone

If I can get straight home before Mamaw
ends her shift & comes in aching to talk,
& before Mom gets home from errands
& wants to know my whole life story.
If I can enter the house in silence.
Heaven. & my whole afternoon gets lifted.
& for an hour, or even two,

I am no longer
Beatrice Miller: Zit Queen
Beatrice Miller: Pariah of the Seventh Grade
Beatrice Miller: Big Head
Beatrice Miller: No Boobs.

I am
Beatrice Miller: Unstoppable
Beatrice Miller: Voted Most Popular + Most Beautiful
+ Most Likely to End Climate Change + Save the World
Beatrice Miller: Perfect-Size Head
Beatrice Miller: Bra wearer.

Sometimes I throw off all my school clothes
& dress up or down. Tank tops
or frilly dresses & I turn up the stereo (yes,
we still have a stereo, since Mamaw thinks

those electronic devices you talk to
try to read your brain—I *think* she's kidding
but I'm not 100 percent sure). So I turn
it all the way up & dance wild around
our house, make miserable amounts
of Kraft mac & cheese. The kind Mamaw
refuses to let me have but Mom stashes
in the garage for when we need it most.
Junk food & sugar highs are necessary
some of the time. & I throw on the TV,
kick my feet up on the couch & pretend
the whole wide world is mine.

When No One Else Is Watching

I transform. Not caterpillar
to butterfly. Or kid to adult.
No metamorphosis for me.
Just me—but way better.
Perfect all my dance moves.
The mirror shows me back
to myself & I look gooooooood.
Get all the steps exactly right.
Sway & dip & rock to the side.
Master the slow groove, slide
& jump back & in again. All
the moves I need, I got 'em.
The freshest, the flyest, most
coolest on the block, in town,
on the planet. I'm magnetic;
people are drawn to me. Popular is what I am when I reflect
back to me. Real & known
& talked about (in a good way).
People see me & flock right
to me. & I know exactly
what to say & how to act
when they arrive.

Searching for Me

Or what it means to be myself, to land.
Today I miss my dad & the way it could have been.
I miss a past I never even knew existed.
Wondering when my life will feel normal.
Oh time. Oh moon that keeps stretching.
Oh sky & pain. Oh mood & disaster.
Oh wishing you alive. Oh breath & time.
Oh ache of muscle. Oh the way you love.
Oh goodbye. Oh sunlight & plants & oxygen.
Oh swing set on a night of sunsets & planets.
Oh planet of my lungs & heart.
Oh blanket of blessings & maple trees
& magnolia & black oak
& all the ways to say I'm needy
& I'm needing. & I need you.
& I'm lost. & there's more world
than you can even imagine.
& it's all there waiting
for me to figure it out.

Voices That Carry Me

Maybe it's because it's just Mamaw, Mom & me.
& their voices feel like song most times. Comforting
& warm. Have always held me close by. Maybe
because their voices are birds & wings & take flight
& fly me home. & most of all. Sound like home.

Could be that's the reason Lucas & Mr. Brady
sound plain old wrong. Disrupt & clunky & cluttered.

I'll speak for . . . What Beatrice was trying to say . . . Oh!
What Beatrice meant by that was . . . She didn't mean . . .

Sometimes their voices feel like stoplights & stop
signs. Blaring red. They sound like sirens sometimes. Slick surrounding me. Silencing me. Too
much & too loud & swamp-like. Overwhelm
& exhaust. Tumbling over me & what I mean.

Mamaw says my dad sounded like wind chimes
& felt like soft breezes on your face swinging in
from the porch. All soothing-like & calm. Says,
"He woulda adored your voice. Held it up high & proud,
shone his love fast & strong on it. Showed it off.
That I can promise you."

Too bad I never heard it in real time.
While he was still alive & mine.

What They Want

Mom wants me dressed up,
skirts & tops, feminine or frilly.
She wants me to look like her
but smaller.

TV shows want me to know it all,
but not say too much. They want
me bossy & aggressive,
but not too much or too loud.
They like to see me from far away.
Sometimes they want me on mute.
The volume all the way down.

Magazines want my imperfections
trimmed up. Legs & armpits shaved
but all the hair in the world on my head.
They use words like "proportional,"
"healthy," "energetic," "the right size for me."

The mall wants me crop topped
& flowery. Flowing & dressed.
They want my belly to show
but only if it's firm & smooth.

100 percent they think they are right.
Want me to work for it.

Promise foundation will disappear
my actual face.
The acne all over it.
Disappear pimples & the way I turn red
when Rodney appears.

The makeup counter
has me thinking lip gloss
will guarantee my smile,
be brighter, better, more
welcoming, that I'll get
a good first kiss but only
if I'm pomegranate puckered
or cherry mint surprised.

Sometimes even Mamaw wants me
on a pedestal. She wants me eccentric
but fitting in, unique but can blend.
Work a cook station, bake cookies,
clean the house top to bottom.

She wants me to be the girl
I'm supposed to be. The one
everyone wants me to be.

But what if I just want to be
me?

Weekend Away

Mom is away
& the house feels empty
without her.
Too quiet
& calm
for both Mamaw & me.

We flip the TV on
sappy love stories
that Mom watches
to fill the space
without
her.

Dear Diary

Look, I know I haven't written in a long time. But now feels like the right moment. I'm kind of lost & feeling more alone than I've ever felt. My mom is on a week-end DATE with a guy who I will call HD (aka the wrong person for her). She just up & left us. Alone. So Mamaw & I have been walking around the house, lost. Trying to find our way without her. I know she wouldn't leave us, but I'm scared. Scared of someone new coming into our lives. When we've lived so long alone. & been perfectly fine without a man. I want my mom happy, but I want Mamaw & me happy too. Is that possible? Also, worst of all—I have an intense crush on a boy who I know doesn't know I'm alive. I mean—he knows, but I don't think he cares. I mean, he might like me as a friend but nothing more. I have no idea. I'm failing in the love department. Mamaw would say, "Buck up, get back in there." Mom would say, "Be the best you that you can be." I like knowing they're both with me, part of my life. I don't want that to change. Not ever.

Yours,

Beatrice Miller

In the Morning

Mom walks in the front door
to find Mamaw & me on the computer.
Both of us hunched over
our big ol' desktop.
We've spent the whole morning
poring over Harrison Douglas
& finding out his life story,
searching his profile
& gawking at photos.
We feel guilty,
but since Mamaw has never
truly googled anything,
it's more a study
in how to understand
how computers work.
She filled her coffee
three times
& is on a caffeine bender.
She started looking at real estate
& owning her own business
& cake recipes
& got on YouTube
to learn about icing
& cookies
& corn bread

& stuffing
& holidays
& life
&&&.

& now she is looking
for a new place to live
& a better job.

We have hit rock bottom
imagining Mom & me
moving to Ohio
with a man
neither of us
likes
one
bit.

Hello

"What are you two doing?" Mom asks,
peering over our shoulders,
looking right at the computer.
"Bea, I have never seen you
sitting there." She moves
to take off her coat.
"Are you looking up apartments?
Where in the world are you going?"

"Well, if you all don't want me,"
Mamaw starts, standing up now,
"then I'd like to find my own way
and my own place to live.
Thank you very much."

"Your own place to live? What?"
My mom looks at me.
"Beatrice, could you give us
a moment?" I retreat to the stairs
so I can still hear everything they say.

"Bea, could you please stop
being so damn dramatic?"

"Well, look who's talking. Ms. Weekend Away,
Ms. Douglas. Ms. Harrison Douglas.

Ms. Whisked Away. Forgot all about us.
Left us here alone."

"Would you give me a break? Please.
Could you let me just be, just figure out
how I want to live the rest of my life?"

"Of course, that's why I'm leaving.
I've thought about it long and hard,
and my being here is dragging you
and Beatrice down. I want you two
to live your lives and be who you want
to be. Without me." I hear Mamaw's
voice choke, & it makes me hold back
my own tears.

"Oh, Bea, we would never leave you,"
I hear Mom say,
"you're our home."

& then I hear what sounds like Mamaw crying,
which is something I hardly ever hear
& then Mom crying
& then I end up sitting on the stairs crying
so Mom and Mamaw hear me
& come to cuddle up close in the stairway.

We are one another's homes,
that is for certain.

"Well, how was your weekend?
I'm guessing we've got to give this
Harrison Douglas
another chance."

Mamaw looks right at me.
I scowl. "I guess."

"I don't think so," my mom says.
"We broke up. I, um . . . I broke up with him.
It's over."

"Oh no, no," Mamaw says. "Well, I'm so sorry."

"You are not. You and Beatrice
weren't going to put up with him
for even a second more.
And to tell you the truth,
neither was I.
Especially when he started critiquing
my parenting skills & how I was raising
my child. Talk about smug."

We all stay silent for a moment,
& then despite the fact that Mom still looks a little upset,
Mamaw jumps up & high-fives me
& starts to shake her hips.

"Well, don't get too excited," Mom says.

But we do, just the same.

"Don't worry," Mamaw says,
"I think I have someone I'd like to set you up with.
I've been doing my own research for you
& trying to find the perfect partner."
This makes me even more nervous
than Harrison Douglas.

"Oh noooo," Mom says,
& we all laugh harder than we have in a long while.

Cover the Plants

First rule of protection
from incoming cold & frost.
Make sure they're comfortable.
Speak to them softly & slowly.
Touch them delicately.
"I know, I know," Mamaw says.
"When people see me
talk to my plants,
tell 'em my life story,
tell 'em how I really feel,
I know what they're thinking.
I'm thinking they're nosy neighbors
but I know they roll their eyes,
call me all kinds of names.
No matter. I imagine
they say it with love
& wish
they could be
as tender
as me."

Inside of Me

Is an everyday wish
to be invited.
Anywhere.

Spend my time
wishing in my bedroom,
seeing myself
somewhere else.

Spend my time
in our tree house
while the weather holds,
bring jackets & blankets.

Places to find myself
while I'm waiting
for everyone else
to find me.

You're Invited

Whispers near my locker,
a list with my name
laced in circling, curling
cursive. The kind
Mamaw wants me
to learn.

Chloe & Brianna
Invite YOU
To a Super Fantastic
Awesome Amazing
Exciting Engaging
Lively Out Loud
Slumber Party!

Place: Chloe's House

What to Bring:
Yourself (ha!)
Pajamas (of course)
Snacks (Chloe & Brianna LOVE hot Takis & chocolate)
Phone
iPad
Laptop

The Cool-ification of Beatrice Miller

It's not easy, not in the least. First,
selfie for real. Raid closet. Only
the rad shirts will survive. Borrow
Mom's push-up bra, red lipstick,
Mamaw's dangly gold drop earrings.
They'd call it stealing. Good thing
they're not home. Lend's more like it.
Purple scarf—check.
Mascara—check,
even though you smear it three times
& have to wash your whole face twice
to start over. Flash. Smile. Show teeth
but not too much. Straighten hair. Hot
iron, gel, de-frizzing spray called Elixir
of Smooth. Says: get the goddess look.
Time to sign up. Try for a ponytail.
Try for a french braid. Try to look serious.
Now bored, now shocked, now quiet
& calm. Now like you just won the lottery.
Because you did. You're in. Invitations
galore. Chloe + Brianna + you
& you are just getting started.
Click. Pose. Snap.

Mamaw Loves Vintage

Or that's what she calls it. I call it plain
old-fashioned Goodwill. Because that's
what it is. And every time we walk
inside, it kind of smells like an attic
in the house of someone who is dead.
"Mamaw, I just don't want to smell like . . ."
She looks at me, always acts so confused
when she doesn't want to hear what I'm saying.
"Death," I whisper, trying to avoid the stares
of the cashiers, who always smile too big,
offer peppermints. "I am not eighty-five years old,
I want to remind them." But Mamaw loves it,
revels in it even. She's only sixty-three, but they give her
the senior deal because her silver hair
puts her over the sixty-five mark in their minds.
"Not my problem if they think a little gray
turns you over-the-hill. I don't mind one bit,"
she says, & I swear she brings her cane
& puts on a little limp just to keep in their good
graces. They cater to her too, bringing her
blouses & slacks (her words) & me old
concert T-shirts. I try & scowl, but Guns
N' Roses is suddenly cool again. So is *Back
to the Future* & *E.T.* & when they bring me
the same puffy green coat with fur collar

I've been studying at the mall, I fold. "Yes,"
I tell Mamaw, hugging it around my body.
She eyes the tag. $75. Still pricey but way less
than the $250 one we saw. She haggles down
to $60, & even I'm impressed. "No one messes
with Mamaw," she says, pulling me & the coat close.
"I can fix that zipper and button in a flash." My first
fancy coat. A real North Coast coat.
Hand-me-down, sure. But mine just the same.

Brown Station Wagon

Circa the gilded age. Circa
the American Revolution. Circa
the age when dinosaurs
roamed the earth. Circa the Ice
Age. Circa forever ago.
Reference: the past. Reference:
history. Back a ways. Aged.
"Come on," I say to Mamaw.
I plead, "Not Brownie," the name
given lovingly (by her) to her Ford
wagon. "Would you rather me
drop you off on the Pink Lady?"
"Your bike?!" I nearly choke
on the ham & cheese biscuit she made me.
Don't be ungrateful. Don't be a jerk.
Don't forget she's your mamaw.
& she woke up early enough
to make your favorite breakfast.
& she loves you enough to give you
a ride in the first place. She smiles.
"I've got an extra helmet, you know."
"Brownie will be just fine," I say.

Cruising

Mamaw & me.
Bluegrass highway heaven.
Rocking, rolling hills.
Radio on blast.
Willie Nelson, Aretha Franklin,
the Pointer Sisters,
Lionel Richie too.
Mamaw's eclectic playlists.
Gotta love it.
& I do.
Windows way down.
Her voice echoes,
wraps around me.
Freeway of love.
All night long.
Natural woman. Wind
winds through us.
"Turn it up!"
Mamaw shouts, laughing.
White picket fences,
dot horse farms,
& sleepy subdivisions.
Sometimes Kentucky's comforting.
& familiar
& warm

& real
& beautiful
& home.

Chloe's House

Is not a house. It's a mansion, sprawling & tall
as it is wide. She's got a pool & its own house

attached in the back. Three-car garage. Circular
driveway that Mamaw meanders into. "Whewww,"

she says, looking around. We've been past here
lots of times on our neighborhood drive-arounds.

I've wished this were mine before. StaceyAnn
& Mariella are doing a sleepover together. Wished

me luck & said they couldn't wait for the stories.
Neither of them cared. I wish I didn't so much.

Somehow, this invitation comes with status. Cool
factor. My name on the list, on the score sheet.

Climbing out from the hole of nonexistence. Rise
up to be considered part of the in crowd. Mamaw

hugs me close, says, "Don't forget to brush your teeth
& wash your face & thank Chloe's family & eat

what you're served. Thank you, & yes ma'am, no
sir, & all that. Don't forget your manners, where

you're from." Hands me a cloth bag of squash,* says never ever show up anywhere empty-handed.

*What do I do with the squash?? Throw it away.

Nice Car

Chloe says when she opens the door
& waves goodbye to Mamaw, who honks
her horn too loud & hollers, "Toodle-oo!"

She's joking, but it doesn't feel that funny
when I see the big SUVs in Chloe's driveway
& the way they take up space in her life.
Breathe.

She takes my coat, even though I want
to keep it on all night. Proud I'm wearing
a North Coast—ready to fit right in.

Chloe squeals when she sees it, says,
"O
M
G.
This is my old coat—from last year!
So awesome! See, it has my initials right here.
Did you get it at Goodwill?!
O
M
G.
My mom takes everything to Goodwill.
It looks so cute on you! I love it. I'm so glad
someone else got some good use out of it."

She puts my coat on a hanger beside
what seems like dozens of new, fluffy
warm coats. She's prepared for anything.

She's not trying to make me invisible.
She's really not. At least, I don't think
she is. But that's exactly the way I feel.

Craft Fair

We spend our day at the Bardstown Craft Fair.
Perfect fall, full of old-timey crafts & new-
wave stands. All of them devoted to Kentucky.
Quilts & homemade everything. Grills fired up
& storefronts open. Downtown is alive,
& wild with people from all over the county.
It's tradition for Mariella & StaceyAnn & me
to go together, so when I see them without me,
I try & avoid them altogether. Think about status
& my place on the planet of middle school.
When they wave, I barely get my hand in the air
before I'm taken in the wave of new friends,
the ones I so wanted to fit in with just days ago.

What We Do

We sail through the crowds.
Order up fries & hot dogs,
grilled burgers with cheese.
Baked is open
& Mamaw is outside in an apron
covered with chocolate sauce
& hot-pink flamingos.
Sunglasses in the shape of martini glasses
perched on her head,
she waves us over,
hands out cherry brownie bars,
introduces herself to everyone
by singing their names.
I roll my eyes fully this time.
Make sure she can see me.

Chloe & Brianna claim space.
Dance through the streets.
I pretend to be that free.
"Let's play truth or dare," they say
& dare me first.
Say how easy it is to take whatever you want
from the stalls. Declare they stole
all they wanted last year.

After being at Chloe's house, I can't imagine
she would ever want anything
she doesn't already have.

Beatrice, We Dare You

My face is flushed when they point to the jewelry stand.
Bluegrass Baubles is what it's called, layered with ruby
rings & necklaces full of rhinestones & colorful beads.
I think about Mamaw & Mom & how they'd see me now,
making conversation, fake laughing & running my
fingers slowly over the glass & gold.
Gems I couldn't afford even if I wanted to.
When the owner helps someone else,
I quickly pull two chunky bands into my palm.
Hold tight
& slide my hand into the tight pocket of my jeans.

"Thanks so much," I call over my shoulder,
speed walking to the group,
who is doubled over at my boldness.
I did it, I mouth to them, hot with excitement & shame.
They smile, tell me they knew I could do it.
"You're one of us now," they say
as I slide both rings onto my fingers.

Slumber Party Drama

Later that night, everyone arrives.
& by everyone, I mean Chloe, Brianna,
Olivia, Eliza, Ebony, Jessica
& of course—me. We hang out upstairs.
Chloe's room (floor) is as big as my whole
house. Her bathroom is a palace unto itself.
Bathtub, separate shower, double sinks.
I am lost in a trance.

It's as if her parents don't exist. They stay
silent. Nod hello & then disappear.
Her older sister is in charge tonight.
She's in the eleventh grade & has pink hair.
I love Chloe's life so much, I can't stand it.

They order us pizza & we turn the TV on,
play YouTube videos on her iPad,
start texting & Snapchatting all at the same
exact time. I pretend I left my devices at home.
I'm dizzy with excitement.

When the doorbell rings two hours later
& Rodney, Noah, Liam & Malik show up,
I am dying. For real. Wish I had a phone
so I could text Mariella & StaceyAnn an SOS!

Send
Help
Fast

Spin the Bottle

Eliza says, closing the door to the basement.
We've moved floors & are now downstairs,
giant movie-screen TV, pool & Ping-Pong table
& no adult anywhere to be found. I want to be
here but want to be home at the same exact time.

I didn't even realize Spin the Bottle was real
or that anyone really played it anymore.
Check my breath in my hand & straighten my hair.
"Scared?" Eliza wants to know, looking us all over.
She's not, that is for sure.

The boys laugh. We make a circle, all of us giddy.
Brianna brings an empty Coke bottle.

"Here are the rules," Eliza says. "The girls spin first.
First boy it lands on goes to the bedroom with them."
"Five minutes in heaven," Ebony says & laughs. I wonder
how she would feel if StaceyAnn were here. I wish
StaceyAnn & Mariella were here.

I've never even been close up enough to smell a boy.
Yuck, my whole existence so far is immature. That
is about to change. I raise my hand (what am I doing?).
"I'll go first," I say, proving how brave I am.

Grab the bottle & give it a turn. It weaves & dances,
lands on Liam.

Liam Hawkins looks up, clearly excited to be first.
The same height as Mariella, he's teased almost as much
as she is. He smiles in my direction, says "let's go"
& walks with me to the bedroom. They all
ooohhhhh & *aaahhhhh* & *awwwww* & *whoaaaaa*.

Questions

How does kissing work?
Who leans in first?
Is it all breath & no breathing?
Or all breathing & no air?
How do I oxygenate?
What is oxygen anyway?
If I don't breathe, how long until I pass out?
Is it possible to look cool while passing out?
What if my breath is a disaster?
Did I eat garlic last night?
Did I eat onions last night?
Who makes the first move?
Do I lean in and smile?
Does he?
Tongue or no tongue?
How is that decided?
& then if our tongues meet,
what do you do with them then?
Movement or no movement?
Breath or breathless?
Breathe or breathing?

Liam + Beatrice = K-I-S-S-I-N-G

We get to the bedroom,
close the door,
stand opposite each other
& stare.
Awwwkkkwardddd.
Liam wears his hair in a ponytail
that rivals Mariella's.
Puts it up, takes it down.
He smiles at me again.
"I've never kissed anyone," he says.
"Me neither."
Silence.
"Spin the Bottle is so stupid," he says.
I know. This whole night
is not the way
I thought it would be.
"Should we kiss anyway?" he asks,
all of a sudden braver than me.
Silence.
Awkward.
Staring.
"I have a crush on Rodney,"
I say,
surprising both myself & Liam.
"Sorry.

But don't tell," I add.

"It's cool," Liam says.

"I have a crush on Amy."

"Chloe's sister?!"

"Yeah, she's only four years older.

Most women like younger men,"

he says, smiling wider.

"Actually, I don't really like

anyone like that.

Not yet at least.

Kissing can wait," he says.

And then: "Rodney is awesome."

"Yeah, I think so too."

Five Minutes Later

We walk out to cheering.
High fives & whoops & hollers.
Did you kiss?
Did you like it?
Tell us everything?

They've already moved on,
ready to play flashlight tag
or jump on the trampoline.
Down soda, play board games,
watch movies.
This game is a joke anyway.

"We didn't," I say.
"Nah," Liam says.
"Scared," Eliza says,
giggling now.
"Beatrice Miller, I like you.
You're just as crazy as your granny."
She's joking too.
But this time,
I know it's not funny.

Mamaw Is a Character

I know it. Mom sure knows it,
since we've been living with her for twelve years now,
& Dad definitely knew it, being her only kid.

& I'll bet he got so many Mamaw-isms,
he could hardly handle it.
'Course, Papaw knew it too,
having been her only love for so long.

So we know. We all know.
Been knowing it our whole lives,
so it's all good to say Mamaw has gone 100 percent
bonkers riding her hot-pink scooter
from the house to Baked,
her portable radio blaring beside her.
Or, oh, there goes Mamaw again in gold pants,
her hair rising like a steeple
from the tip-top of her head.
Carrying on with what she calls her gal pals.
Hooting & hollering to town.

We know she's kooky & wily. Her words & sayings.
& that she dances when she's s'posed to be sitting,
cuts up when it's serious. Cool. We get it.
It's when other people say so that I start to get angry.

So when Eliza says,
"Yeah, your grandmother is CRAZY,"
I don't know, but something snaps loose inside me.
Because the word "crazy" is not a cool word,
or a kind one,
or a funny one.

It's just plain old mean.
& all of a sudden, I get it.
I'm so tired of being surrounded by so much stuck up—
& think maybe they are too.
I resist the urge to sock Eliza in her perfectly
contact-lensed blue eye & pull my arm all the way back.

But even after knowing I should walk away, I stay.
Instead of speaking up for Mamaw, I laugh right along.
Say, "Yeah, she's totally out of it. So weird and kooky,"
hating myself for not sticking up for her.

Inside, I am aching, wish I could say how I really feel.
I want to say—"She's not my grandmother;
she's my mamaw, and the only one I've ever known.
I love all of her. & I'd never call her crazy.
I'd never use that word on anyone—or use it to put
anyone down. And I've got way more stories
from living my life with her than you'll probably
ever have. I'm really lucky she's mine."

Instead I just stay silent—laughing the loudest
right along with them.

Tag

The tears are hot & exhausted
when they wash down my face.
"Feel like I've been crying forever,"
I say to no one & the hills. Let out
a sigh. My stomach feels full
of salty pepperoni pizza & doubt.
The way a night can change
from perfect to disaster
in a second's time. One blink,
a breath let out. My skin is cold
against the dew. Is flashlight tag
really a game if you don't get caught?
If no one ever even finds you?
My legs feel gummy, achy even,
as if I've been running, been chased,
& let's be clear. I have not been.
I come to the neighborhood's end.
The streetlight centers a spotlight
until I realize it's the glow of a flashlight.
& standing behind the shine is Rodney.

You're It

His face is lit up & glowing. "Oh,"
I say, internally kicking myself.
Why can't I ever say the right things?
"You're it,"
he says, and just when I think:
Game
Over
he stops. "Are you okay?" he asks.
Why is he always asking that?
Why am I always not okay?
Getting closer, his flashlight warm
on my skin. "No," I say, wiping my eyes
& trying to keep my head low.
"Yeah, this game sucks," he says,
walking my way & sitting beside me,
sharing space on the edge of the driveway.
The air is too cold for this game.
"I can't go back there," I say suddenly,
surprising myself & Rodney, who looks up
fully, nothing else to distract him.
No computer or phone—nothing lighting
his face besides his flashlight. Just me,
& maybe he can see right through.

What Rodney Says

"I feel that way sometimes too.
Like I don't belong. None of us
really does. Least. That's how I feel."

& even though I still feel alone,
it's like there's someone with me,
right beside me. Because there is.

Scared & unknown. Outside
of the inside circle. Sometimes.
But tonight. That feels all right.

We Stay Talking

For what feels like forever.
I'm wishing we could go back,
spin the bottle one more time.
I'd like another chance.

I say:
"Seventh grade is harder than I thought.
Being twelve is harder than I thought.
My birthday is next weekend.
My mamaw is taking me to a hotel for the night,
so at least there's that to look forward to.
Do you think thirteen will be better?"

He says:
"Seventh grade is not as bad as sixth grade.
My birthday was over the summer.
I'm already thirteen.
It's pretty much the same."

We both start to laugh,
& just like that, we're in the same boat
together—both of us just drifting along.

The Next Day

Keep my secrets
close beside me

Spin the Bottle
Stealing the rings
Crying the tears
Laughing at Mamaw
Laughing at me
In the past
Hug Mamaw hard
Hide the truth
Almost thirteen now
Horizon is clear
Don't tell anyone
Your true self
Rearview mirror

Fancy Hotel Birthday Weekend

It's a tradition since I was ten
& asked Mom & Mamaw
if we could go to the Bluegrass Inn
to sleep in silky sheets in big ol'
king-size beds, order room service
& play tag in the heated indoor pool.
We usually stay only one night
& savor as much as we possibly can,
treat ourselves to snacks & games
& endless cable TV. But this time,
Mamaw said she splurged
& we could stay the whole weekend.
Just the two of us on Friday night
& then Mom arriving on Saturday
after her shift. At least one night
where we can all kick back & relax
together.

I try to make all the plans. Excited
for the hour-long drive, radio on,
hot-tub jets & jumping from cold
to hot over & over again. Loads
of soda, salty snacks & every treat
you can imagine. This weekend
is supposed to be the best one ever.

Turning thirteen—almost a woman.
But my stomach turns, thinking
& spinning about the Beatrice
I showed off to my new friends.
It didn't seem like me at all.
Ashamed of what I did to prove myself.
Try to stop my mind from racing,
push it away. Keep pretending,
keep it all tucked safe inside,
keep making believe
I know exactly what I'm doing.

Hotel Pools

"Underwater is not just weightless, it's *divine*."
That's a Mamaw word if I ever heard one.
She uses it to describe her corn bread with honey,
her maple-bacon cupcakes, or the sweet time
she gets alone at home when Mom & I leave
her peace & quiet. That's how I feel now.
Fall break, birthday weekend. Vacation swim
is my favorite kind. The smell of chlorine.
Hazy & thick with steam.
Mamaw calls directions.
Dive, handstand, backstroke, freestyle, splits,
cannonball.
She sits in the hot tub with me. Leans way back
& sighs. "This is the life," she sings. & she's right.
Without my goggles, I can't see the world
around me is a drifting mystery. No shapes
or hard angles. Just floating, just free.

Order Up

Mamaw says after the microwave beeps. Hot
Kraft macaroni & cheese bubbles to the top.
She stays slicing bologna into squares for me,
laying on top of saltine crackers doused in Louisiana
hot sauce. Cracks open the plastic of American
cheese. Salty goodness. So much savory sodium,
she says, she'll wake up with swollen hands.
"Not a care," Mamaw says, buttering her bread.
"Vacations are for bad food, swimming pools,
extra cholesterol, extra calories, extra pure
joy. Cable TV turned on all the wrong channels
& you & me. Curled up soaking it all in."

Happy Birthday, Beatrice

Last night of vacation.
Mom arrives finally.
Throws shoes off.
Cuddles us close.
Mamaw unwraps cookies.
Chocolate chip walnut.
Fancy new journal.
Fancy new pens.
Fancy new book.
Fancy new bookmark.
Marking my life.
Thirteen feels babyish.
Somehow still lost.
Say thank you.
Don't say scared.
Don't say lost.
Don't say alone.
Don't start crying.
Don't lose control.
Hold the truth.
Trying so hard
to stay above,
eyes tearing up,
hold it in,
breath & all.

Don't lose control.
Hold the truth.
Can't stop now.

End of Vacation Life

Some days I wake up & I'm all sunshine.
All helium-filled balloons & dance parties.
Music turned up all the way.

But some days, I wake up & I'm thunderstorms.
Heat lightning—my whole self feels heavy & clunky
& unreliable. That's how I feel today.

So I pull the covers tighter around me.
Try to be a cocoon
or my own life raft. Ignore the way my heart
is attempting to slip out of my body.

That's how Mamaw finds me. Steaming cup of cocoa
from the lobby downstairs between her hands.
"Bug" & "flowerpot" & "lemon drop" is what she calls me.
Throws the shades open.

Tells me you can't quit before you even start.
Wipes my eyes with her wrinkled hands.
Holds me still & calm.
Rocks me steady & ready & awake.

Sometimes in My Dreams

I am in the highest swing
on the swing set
& make every goal
& slam dunks are my life.
In real life,
I don't even like sports
but dream gold medals,
the tallest trophies, ribbons.
The saying: "people choke on my dust"
is true
because I'm not just fast,
I'm a train straight
off the rails,
one hundred miles an hour.
The way Mamaw
drives when she's full of fury.
The ways she says
she drove the night they called
to tell her my dad
(her son) died.
But in my dreams,
I am not full
of sadness like a lost boat.
Death is not my only story.
I am a fireball,

firecracker,
fired up
& other things that burn.
I kick the ball highest,
my legs the strongest.
The sheer amount
of push-ups I can finish in a minute
is straight-up bonkers.
Iron Woman.
Unstoppable.
Mind-numbingly powerful
& athletic
& so skilled at
e v e r y t h i n g
that other folks take notes.

But sometimes—
even in my dreams.
I don't make it out alive.
I just sink
deeper
& deeper
& deeper
until
I

disappear.

Dreaming Another Me

California dreams
far away as possible
could I disappear?

Imagine mountains
homes that don't belong to me
new identity.

Run, run, run away
been singing myself to sleep
but when I wake up

I'm still here.

The Way Home

Mamaw turns the volume
up high. Rolls the windows
all the way down. Riding
through a wind tunnel.
Says the cold air opens
your pores. Sings top volume
Sam Cooke & Loretta Lynn.
Mom belts it out too,
the two of them
conspiring against me.
Put my headphones on,
sound all the way up.
Feeling good finally,
no worries at all,
like I finally got away
with it. Thinking
maybe my days
of worrying are over,
so I kick back,
put my hands over
my headphones
& rock.

That's when Mamaw
looks through the rearview

& must see the glint
off my fake diamonds
flurry in the mirror.
She says, "My goodness,
those look just exactly
like Bluegrass Bauble."
Gaudy in sun-
light, they shine.
In an instant,
I remember, sliding
them on my fingers
this morning, full
of myself. "Oh!
My new friends,
they bought them
for my birthday," I explain,
rolling them around.
"Pretty pricey gift,"
Mamaw says, shutting
off the radio & looking
even closer at me & my lie.

Arrival

I'm unpacking the weekend
when Mamaw shows up
in my doorway. Tells me
she's disappointed. Says,
"Beatrice Miller,
I've never known you
to tell a tall tale,
but I just got off the phone
with Misty Cole.
& you know what?
She told me no young girls
bought one lick of jewelry
from her stand last weekend.
Fact is, she said someone
stole something special
from her. Described them
& everything. Gold-&-gem-
filled rings. Fancy & shiny
ones you couldn't miss.
Described the ones
I saw in the mirror
on the way home."

I Stole Them

"Big deal," I say
& regret it instantly.
Mamaw is never
that mad. All Zen-like
& calm. She's smooth
& laid-back, but now
she gets to shouting.
Says it's high time
I apologize to her
& Mom, who's standing
in the doorway.
"Spoiled & acting out,
can't even tell
who it is
you're trying to be.
Can't even
recognize you,"
Mamaw says.

"Well, I'm standing
right here," I shout,
mad at myself now.
Start packing my bag,
keep both stolen rings
tight around my fingers.

Mad at my life
& Mamaw & all her magic
feel-good-ness.
& Mom for working so hard
but still not making enough,
& me for feeling worthless
sometimes & not enough too.
& myself again
for being a brat & a baby
& most of all at my dad
who left me too fast
& too soon
& who I miss today
& always
& now I'm mad
at my tears
& the way they slide
reckless
down my face.
Embarrassed
that I can't even
be thankful
for what I have.
Storm downstairs,
slam the screen door
& ride.

Tree House

Zoom through the back roads
ignore the rushing cool wind
make it in record time.

Peel back the tree bark
sit in our makeshift hammock
& rock myself slow.

Who have I become
I'm not recognizable
to people I love.

Zip my jacket up
close my eyes & say a prayer
hope Mamaw hears me.

Apology

I must have fallen asleep
because when Mariella & StaceyAnn
pull up on their bikes,
they scare the bejesus
out of me.

"AHHHHHHHHHHH!!!
Holy crap," I shout.

"Jeez," StaceyAnn says. "Calm down."
"Yeah," Mariella adds. "It's just us."
"You don't recognize us?" StaceyAnn asks,
cocking her hip & smirking at me.
"Remember us? We are, or, we *were*
your best friends."

"I'm so sorry," I say, suddenly aware
of how cold it is. The tip of my nose
frozen. Face still wet from crying.
"I messed up. Trying to be someone
I'm not."

"We don't forgive you," StaceyAnn says.
Mariella nudges her. "Yes, we do. Just

don't do it again. Act like you know us
next time. & get up," Mariella says.
"You gotta get home. Your mamaw.
She's been texting me like wild.
& she's really bad at texting."

Texts from Mamaw (from My Mom's Phone)

Mrlla—cme gt Bea

Dang phne—not know txt

Crppp—phone—cant get no

Wherrrr s Beatriceeee??? Dangitt

Call bck. Npw.

Text from Mom

Come home
Sweet Beatrice
Come home

My Heart

Longing
& ruin
& pummel
& ache
& joy
& wishing
& pumping
& glowing
& flowering
& peeling
& hot pink
& blazing
& missing
& full
& rising
& trembling
& awake
& here
& far away
& inside
& glowing
& yours
& mine
& alive.

Poem of Forgiveness

You see me
& I'm enough.
I know this.
Sometimes I ache
figuring myself out
missing my dad
missing his life
could have been
might have been.

Sometimes I'm ashamed
of our life
& our garden
& our house
& my clothes
& our computer
& no phone
& your eccentricities,
I say, cringing
but being honest.

But most times
I love it
& you both.
Wouldn't want it

any other way.
I'm a jerk
& I'm sorry.
I'm so sorry.

They hold me
in a hug
so tender & long,
that I appear
back to me.
See myself new
taking up space
being the girl
I was always
meant to be.

Truth Is

Mamaw starts in, looking straight at me,
"While you know I always appreciate a good
old-fashioned *I'm Sorry*, you & I both know
that's not enough. I nod. It's been that way
since I was a kid. Every time I messed up,
or made a mistake, Mamaw or Mom
(or both of them) would tell me
I had to make it right & most of the time
I had to figure it out on my own.

"Good thing I know Ms. Cole. Don't worry.
I'm sure she's made a few mistakes too.
I'm betting she'll understand. Now get to it,"
Mamaw says, pulling out the basket of notecards
that sits on her desk.
"Don't worry about all that fancy
cursive lettering this time.
Just tell the truth,
just speak from here," she says,
putting her hand above my heart.
"That's all that ever matters anyway."

& all of a sudden, I know she's right.

Dear Ms. Cole

I messed up. It was all me.
Seventh grade is way harder
than I thought it would be.
I stole the rings last Saturday.
Both of them.
All I wanted was to fit in
& have people see me as popular,
have them see me & wish
they could be friends with me.
Laugh at all my jokes,
wanna hang out with me,
ride bikes, work on my treehouse.
I'm not gonna lie,
I took those rings
so people would look at me
in a different way,
& when I showed them what I did,
I felt a kind of liftoff.
Floating.
They could see how wild
& daring I was.
But afterwards, all I did was deflate.
Out of air.
It felt like I'd have to keep taking risks
to just stay in their spotlight.

& then I felt guilty
& embarrassed
that I even wanted that so bad
in the first place.
Felt sick to think
I'd let someone else
make me feel not good enough
or not in place enough.
I'm sorry I stole the rings.
I thought they'd turn me into someone else.
I even wanted that.
But now I realize that being anyone other than myself
is the biggest mistake I could ever make.
Please give me the chance to pay for the rings
by helping out in your gallery this winter.
Thank you for considering.

Sincerely,

Beatrice Miller

One More Apology

Mom reads the letter
before I seal the envelope.
She smiles, while tears fill her eyes
& pulls me toward her.
"You know, my folks had me working
from the time I turned twelve.
Babysitting, helping around the house,
you name it, I was doing it.
Laundry, gardening, dishes.
Didn't have much time for friends
or fooling around. I had to be tough.
By sixteen, I had two jobs,
and in college, forget about it.
I just worked and worked.
It was all I knew.
And then your dad died.
After you were born
I just threw myself into work
even more. Worked to forget
and worked to give myself
something to do, ease my mind.
I guess somehow, along the way
I forgot what it was like to be a kid
and sometimes
I want you to grow up too fast,

to work too hard—just like me.
But I see you with StaceyAnn and Mariella
and Mamaw
and I see you laughing
and just enjoying your life
and working hard to help us
all at the same time
and I try to remember that you're twelve."

"Thirteen now," I remind her.

"That's right. Yes. Thirteen.
I want to say I'm sorry too.
For sometimes asking too much of you,
too fast. I've been thinking that sometimes
it helps to just get out of the way
and give you the space you need," Mom says,
& as soon as she does, I pull her close.

"Don't go too far though. Please?"

She holds me tight next to her,
& we stay that way until morning.

Friendsgiving

Mamaw & Mom
invite the whole block.
Our house stays open
for Friendsgiving.
Mamaw's favorite holiday.
Fried turkey & Tofurky
for days.
Stuffing with sausage
& sage. Lemony
pound cake & cookies
made with rolled oats
& raisins, dark chocolate
& walnuts. Cranberry
sauce & green beans
loaded with ham hock.
Mariella's family
brings *elote* & they help
make our house a feast.
StaceyAnn's mom
& dad join us,
whip up mashed potatoes
& savory gravy.
Red-velvet cake
& lemon meringue
& coconut cream

& Shirley Temples
we mix with maraschino
cherries & sweet juice.
Another birthday cake
& more candles. Mom
invites her coworkers
& Mamaw invites hers
too. Along with a special
someone she thinks
Mom will like. The house
full & smelling like sautéed
onions & garlic all day.
Mariella & StaceyAnn
want all the scoop. Say
I better be there for them
at StaceyAnn's birthday
at the roller-skating rink.

Join Mamaw in giving thanks,
say a silent one for friends
who love me
exactly the way I am.

Mamaw Dancing Was So Beautiful

It near made me cry. & I would have.
Had there not been a whole Friendsgiving
crowd staring & standing in her sway.

She was all casual & catapult.
Smooth & shoulders.
Sunset & banjo.
Hips & hilltops.

With everyone watching. Eyes
wide. She reached out to me.
& I went ahead & joined her.
Twirling & bumping. Shaking
& erasing all the ideas other folks
might've had of me & us & all
I was & am capable of. Yeah,
I went ahead & shook
till I couldn't shake
no more.

What Money Can't Buy

Feeling this full.
A cool November night,
singing songs together,
porch sitting, still holding hands.
All of us & a bonfire in the yard.
S'mores soon or something
to satisfy sweet teeth.
My mom's voice lifting
me right up.
The garden still alive,
not quite frozen over
just yet. The earth
& the people
who love me
still beating
& pulsing
around me.

Reasons Mariella & StaceyAnn Are Forever Friends

In first grade, I wet my pants in the bathroom.
Mariella found me crying & rushed to ask for help.
She brought a change of clothes & stayed with me
talking me down from my elementary school panic
& never told one other person about it.

In third grade, Joey Blane said his dad knew my dad
& said my dad was a good-for-nothing. I knew enough
to cry & tell the teacher, who said she couldn't prove it.
StaceyAnn believed me anyway & socked him in the jaw.
She got a week's detention from recess. I sat inside
with her every single day.

In fourth grade, we perfected our dance routine to every
single Beyoncé song. Entrances & exits. We recorded
our future YouTube videos—gave ourselves new names.
I was Crystal, StaceyAnn was Rebel,
& Mariella was Queen.

In fifth grade, we wrote a zine called: *Country Stories*
& wrote down all the tallest tales
we'd heard from family.
We put on a production of: *Bardstown Secrets*
& pretended we lived in a ghost town. Set up scavenger
hunts, built whole cities with dolls & blocks.

Spent all our days together.

In sixth grade, we crowned ourselves the Social Misfits.
Then it didn't matter who liked who & who had a crush
on who. What mattered was making each other laugh,
the best food from the best garden,
Mariella's family's restaurant,
StaceyAnn's dad's dirt bike.
Our families & the ways they all held us.

What matters now is I get it. Know the truth
& how to hold friends as close as possible.
As long as possible.

Girls Are Bad Drivers—Part I

"No way," I say, my mouth
full of pepperoni pizza.
"You should see my mamaw.
The way she takes corners
& hills, she . . ." I look up,
see everyone watching me.

On the inside, the conversation goes something like this:
What is wrong with you, Beatrice Miller?!
Did you just bring up your granny
in a conversation at StaceyAnn's
birthday party
when everyone else is steady drinking soda
& being normal everyday seventh graders?
Are you bonkers? Did you just brag
about the way your mamaw takes corners?!
AHHHHHHHHHHH!

Silence.

On the outside:
"Oh, I just mean, uh, she's
really fast is all. And, uh, a really
great driver. That's all I meant.
Like, she could beat you in a race."

Inside: *Why are you still talking?*
Shut up, Beatrice. Seriously.

Outside: "Also, that's a total stereotype
to say that all girls are bad drivers.
& it's not true. At all. Fact is my mamaw
could beat you at any race."

Inside: *NOOOOOOO!!!!!*

Lucas starts laughing, says,
"I'd beat your granny any ol'
day. And I've been in the car
with my mom & my sister
& my grandma. What I said
is true. Girls Are Bad Drivers."

Prove It

StaceyAnn says. She's listening
in behind me. Fired up for sure.
She's been go-karting
& motorbiking & tractor-ing
since she was nine & cruising
on the back of motorcycles
with her dad & her mom.
Not scared of any highway
or back road. If I was in trouble,
I'd all the time want StaceyAnn
riding along beside me.
& she beats us all at *Grand Prix*.
Swears her mom said she'd teach
her in the school parking lot
after the eighth grade. "A woman
should know how to drive
a stick shift & an automatic,"
she's all the time saying.
So I know a good challenge
when I see one. & I know that Lucas
(who was only invited
because StaceyAnn's mom
insisted they invite the whole class)
is going down.

Girls Are Bad Drivers—Part II

Lucas says it again
right before StaceyAnn
CRUSHES
his score at *Grand Prix Legends*.
It's easily
the sweetest defeat
I've ever seen.
We all whoop & shout.
I'm not positive
but I think Rodney yells loudest.
My snow cone nearly flips
out of my hand, & Mariella
skates straight out on the rink,
raises her arms to the disco ball,
& shouts, "YEAHHHHHHH."
She knows a win when she sees one.
The DJ (also our gym teacher)
plays "Last Night a DJ Saved My Life"
by Indeep & we know this
because he keeps shouting
the lyrics into the microphone.
StaceyAnn pulls back & hugs me
around the neck. "I won,"
she whispers. "She won!" I shout,
smiling hard at Lucas.

He kicks the machine & it sings,
"W-w-w-WIPE OUT!"
As if on cue, as if the whole
roller-skating rink
is in on the joke.
He sulks down low
in his chair. Tries to say
"do-over," but no one
hears him over our voices
all rising up over him
& his old-fashioned
ideas.

Berry Teaches Us Self-Love & Worth—
Lesson One Trillion

She
tells us:
write our dreams
vision future
selves & how to soar
take it seriously
never underestimate you
& all you're capable of now
they'll try & tell you girls don't know how
change their perceptions just by showing up
Shift the way they see you, show yourself off
pride is only ugly if you're lost
or bragging out of turn; you're not
show them the Beatrice I see
the one you keep hiding
one you've stowed away
scared of yourself
don't let them
define
you

Beatrice Miller's Abecedarian

Always
Believing
Crying
Dreaming
Every
Fantasy
Gargantuan
Hypnotizing
Inspiring
Jarring
Kaleidoscope
Laughable
Magic
Natural
Obsessive
Perfectionist
Quirky
Rambunctious
Soaring
Talkative
Understanding
Verse
Wacky
Xenodochial
Young
Zany

Winter on Its Way

Rain
won't stop,
pours endless
from above, makes
me hold all my breath
& count every minute
& replay every second.
All of me is crying inside,
feels so much like outside, I open
my windows & put my face to the sky.

Mamaw Says

Walking empties your brain,
so we keep at it. Sometimes
with weights on both ankles
& two-pounders in our palms.
She keeps up a speed
that has me huffing & puffing.
"Pump those legs, Beatrice.
Work those biceps.
Use that core.
A good heart
is one that lasts
& keeps on ticking
& tick-tick-ticking."
Know she's thinking
of Papaw & how his heart
gave on out. Up & stopped
on her & us.
We hoof it on straight
through the cemetery,
kiss our palms & offer
our own healthy hearts
& lungs. "Gotta remember
even when they're gone,"
she says. Then: "Pick up
the pace." Circle the block,

school parking lot. She loves
to run laps around town,
then the football field
& up & down the bleachers.
If you think grandmas
are old & lazy,
then you definitely haven't met mine.
She teases me while doing squats.
Pumps her arms in victory.
Laps me & giggles.
After a while, I let her.
Tell her I need a water break.
Lean back on the bottom bleacher
& feel the almost winter sun
wash over my face.
When I open my eyes,
I see Rodney Murphy
looking right back at me.
& changing the whole
shape of my day.

What's Up

Rodney says, shading his eyes with his palm.
I'm still breathing harder than I should be.
He looks up to the top of the bleachers,
Kentucky's sunshine reflecting back from his silver
sunglasses. I stay squinting up at him.
And you can't miss Mamaw,
who's wearing her neon-green biker pants
& exercise cape, which she assured me was in fashion
but I'm beginning to think
she just cut the arms off an old sweatshirt,
fanned it out in the back
& then extended the truth so's I wouldn't say anything.
She's singing at the top of her lungs.
"I got a new attitude." We both smile.
"So that's your mamaw, huh?"
"Well, nobody else would claim her," I say
& instantly feel guilty, even though I know
she'd laugh at that too.
I know Rodney is thinking about what Eliza said
& the word "crazy" is probably right at the top
of his tongue too, but he just looks at her
& then back at me.

Says, "I think 'eccentric' is a good word for her."
"Yeah, me too," I say.

"Also 'wild' and 'unique' and 'super special'
and 'one of a kind.'"

"Yeah," he says,
"kind of like you."

The Color of Tomatoes—

Is what I turn
when Rodney says this.
The petite ones we plant
in our side garden.
Ultimate red-faced,
I start to say "thank you"
but then hear footsteps
barreling down the middle.
"Is that Rodney?" she loud-whispers in my ear.
"I can hear you," he says,
& they both laugh. *What is happening?*
"Mamaw, meet my friend Rodney.
Rodney, this is Mamaw, my grandma."
"Who is sometimes mistaken
for Beatrice's sister and sometimes
mistaken for her great-grandma.
I am what you call a shape-shifter."
"An original," Rodney says,
& Mamaw & I both smile.
Mamaw says, "You know what
I could use after a good workout?
A cupcake," she answers herself.
"And I know just the place.
Rodney? Join us?"

And That's How We End Up

We help ice two dozen
double-chocolate cupcakes,
our gloved hands working
double-time at Baked
while Mamaw hums, turns
the radio up & bounces
from countertop to stove.
The kitchen smells so sweet,
I almost think I'll pass out.
Can't tell if it's the sugar
or the way my heart
is bump, bump, bumping
in my chest. This falling
for someone. Is as much
a workout. As running
up all those steps. Feels
as good to me as all
that blood pumping,
arm raising, jumping-
jack doing & speed
walking combined.

The Walk Home

Rodney doesn't hold my hand
but bumps into me twice, gentle
& easy. Says he's sorry about score
sheets & Spin the Bottle. Says he'd love
to hang out sometime. Talk comic books
& ice cream flavors. He'd love to grow a garden,
something from the earth. At my doorway, I lean in,
surprising myself & Rodney both. Is this what
firecrackers feel like? My mouth is a field of strawberries.
It's a tree swing flying to the clouds. Or clouds too full
to the bursting point of rain. Pouring.
I'm lit up—a skyline of some city I've never visited
or seen but can imagine. New York or Chicago.
That's how I feel inside. Yes. That's how I imagine
my heart feels inside too. Kissing for the first time,
a fresh, new magic.

When I Can't Sleep—Episode 4.592

Walk
all night
through my mind
so cavernous
I nearly get lost
imagine myself whole
striding into school so cool
I nearly glide across the surface
people watch me & say, *who's that girl*
did we just meet, is she new, what's her name?

Can't believe I'm the same Beatrice as old
like some new, shiny bold; I'm like gold
I shimmer when they look my way
don't shy from their attention
I go on, soak it all in
let them praise the new me
when they ask, *Beatrice?*
I just say, *yes*
you missed me
the first
time.

Happy New Year

Mamaw whispers in my ear
& I actually believe it will be.
The three of us sit outside,
Mamaw, Mom & me,
the way it has always been.
We let all the stars & all the sky shine
& all the dust of the earth
& all the planets
& all the matter
& all that matters
watch over us.

Atmosphere & design—however life
decides to unfold. Mom is home
for tonight. Cradling & holding us.
We have already devoured her lentil soup,
loaded with sweet carrots & potatoes,
lemon meringue pie piled tall as a tower.
We've already laid out all our crystals
& written our wishes on tiny slivers
of paper, burying them deep into the soil
for next year. Mamaw's got so many sayings,
sometimes I can't hardly keep them straight
in my brain.
But I've got the feeling this one's
going to stick with me.

She says, "You've got to nurture and tend
and water and cradle and pay close attention
to your dreams. Let them rise up
and grow out of control.
Let them lead the way always."

She sits back in her favorite chair,
pulls out some blankets from the shed.
I almost ask to sit in her lap
or burrow into Mom's,
but tonight
I feel strong somehow
starting on my own.
Feel like I can plant my own life and watch it grow.
I settle for holding both their hands.

Consider myself forever lucky.
For a Kentucky sky above me,
almost snow, a house that's warm
with a fire & quilts & arms that know
how to hug & hold & let go,
from all the memories of a dad
who loved me so hard, for a mom
who loves me endlessly,
for my friends who are family,
& especially & always for a granny
like Mamaw, who manages to make magic

the everyday, makes me magic
just for being loved by her.
"Happy New Year," I say back.
"To all the things we wish for
& all the ways to make them happen."

Acknowledgments

Always thankful for the community of friends & artists who make this world shine, shine. Forever grateful for: Grisel Y. Acosta, Stephanie Dionne Acosta, Juan Acosta, Lisa Ascalon, Jennifer Baker, Julia Berick, Dan Bernitt, Berry, Tokumbo Bodunde, Marc Boone, Lori Brown-Niang, Susan Buttenwieser, Moriah Carlson, Olivia Cole, Angie Cruz, Bobby DeJesus, Jessica Diaz, Mitchell L. H. Douglas, Jason Duchin, Dana Edell, Kelly Norman Ellis, John Ellrodt, Maria Fico, Rajeeyah Finnie-Myers, D. A. Flores, Kevin Flores, Marsha Flores, Asha French, Tanya Gallo, Aracelis Girmay, Nanya-Akuki Goodrich, Catrina Ganey, Rachel Eliza Griffiths, Andrée Greene, Lisa Green, Ysabel Y. Gonzalez, Jake Hagan, Jen Hagan, Lisa Hagan, Michael Hagan, Karen Harryman, Lindsey Homra, Melissa Johnson, Amanda Johnston, Parneshia Jones, Carey Kasten, Caroline Kennedy, Michele Kotler, Mino Lora, Tim Lord, Rob Linné, Veronica Liu, Will Maloney, Alison McDonald, Stacy Mohammed, Kamilah Aisha Moon, Andrea Murphy, Alecia Whitaker, Willie Perdomo, Andy Powell, Sarina Prabasi, Danni Quintos, Emily Raboteau, David Reilly, Carla Repice, Kate Dworkoski Scudese, Pete Scudese, Vincent Toro, Natalia Torres, Alondra Uribe, Jessica Wahlstrom, Crystal Wilkinson, Jenisha Watts & Marina Hope Wilson.

Growing up in Bardstown, Kentucky, gave me a crew of

amazing friends. We grew through so much together. I will forever be thankful for how they showed up & how we grew up to hold & carry each other. Leslie Hibbs Blincoe, Becca Christensen, Megan Clark Garriga, Britt Kulsveen, Brandi Cusick Rimpsey, Lisa Forsee Roby, Melanie Ballard Sewell, Kate Carothers Smith & Kelly Wheatley.

Elma's Heart Circle & all the women who are a home for me. So many of these poems started in this writing group. So grateful to be a part of this beautiful community. Cheryl Boyce-Taylor especially & always, & this sisterhood of poets: E. J. Antonio, Cheryl Clarke, LeConté Dill, Kathy Engel, JP Howard, Caits Meissner, Yesenia Montilla & Christina Olivares.

Renée Watson for your friendship & feedback & heart & guidance through my first middle grade novel in verse. Thank you!

To my early readers: Rob Linné, Renée Watson & Kelly Wheatley—thank you for your comments & questions & all the love.

Sarah Shumway Liu—I loved the way you saw Beatrice Miller. Thank you for caring so deeply for this story & for your sharp editorial eye & the heart you bring to this work.

Thank you to the team at Bloomsbury: Erica Barmash, Alexa Higbee, Beth Eller, Jasmine Miranda & Lily Yengle—for ushering Beatrice into the world.

Rosemary Stimola—thank you for your vision &

brilliance. It is such a joy to work with you & the entire team at Stimola Literary Studio.

Deb Shapiro & Shreve Williams for the amazing care & attention to this book.

For the family collectives that helped to raise me as a writer & educator & activist: Affrilachian Poets, Alice Hoffman Young Writers Retreat at Adelphi University, Café Buunni, Conjwoman, The DreamYard Project, Dodge Poetry Festival, girlstory, GlobalWrites, International Poetry Exchange Program, Kentucky Governor's School for the Arts, New York Foundation for the Arts, Northern Manhattan Arts Alliance, Northwestern University Press, People's Theatre Project, Sawyer House Press, and VONA.

For my parents—always. Gianina & Patrick Hagan for allowing me to be as reckless & as glorious as I wanted and tried to be. Thank you always.

For my partner—David Flores. Your work holds me up. What a joy to be in this world making art together. Love—always.

Finally to my daughters—Araceli Miriam Hagan Flores & Miriam Elinor Hagan Flores. You make me want to create work that makes you proud & that matters in the world. I love you both endlessly.